Sky pointed toward the mountains.

"I need to be up there for a while," he said.

"Why not go up by yourself?"

"I thought it might be more fun to go with you. You've never been packing before, you don't know a thing about horses and you're a city dude."

"I'm being typecast," Elaina complained jokingly.

He shook his head. "You're looking forward to this with all the excitement of a kid at Christmas, and I want to watch you open your presents. I'm counting on you to be awed."

"And awkward, ignorant and tenderfooted."

She smiled at him, and he felt his stomach tighten. How long had it been since he'd known that feeling? Dipping his head closer to her ear, he added quietly, "And natural. And so damn pretty it makes my throat go dry."

"Good line, Mr. Hunter." She managed a light tone, but she wanted to believe that his throat *was* dry and that his insides fluttered just the way hers did.

Dear Reader:

Romance readers have been enthusiastic about the Silhouette Special Editions for years. And that's not by accident: Special Editions were the first of their kind and continue to feature realistic stories with heightened romantic tension.

The longer stories, sophisticated style, greater sensual detail and variety that made Special Editions popular are the same elements that will make you want to read book after book.

We hope that you enjoy this Special Edition today, and will enjoy many more.

Please write to us:

Jane Nicholls
Silhouette Books
PO Box 236
Thornton Road
Croydon
Surrey
CR9 3RU

KATHLEEN EAGLE
Carved in Stone

Silhouette Special Edition

Originally Published by Silhouette Books
a division of
Harlequin Enterprises Ltd.

First published in Great Britain in 1987 by Silhouette Books, Eton House, 18–24 Paradise Road, Richmond, Surrey TW9 1SR

© Kathleen Eagle 1987

Silhouette, Silhouette Special Edition and Colophon are Trade Marks of Harlequin Enterprises B.V.

ISBN 0 373 50720 8

23–1187

Printed and bound in Great Britain by Cox & Wyman Ltd, Reading

To: Kay, Judy, Sandy, Barb, Julie, Barb and
Andy, whose foot was an inspiration.
For all my women friends,
because "the people are not defeated until
the hearts of their women are on the ground."

KATHLEEN EAGLE

is both a writer and a teacher, whose experiences in
each profession continue to enrich her enjoyment of
the other. She is presently serving as president of the
North Dakota Council of Teachers of English, and
has discovered that giving up what she likes least—
housework—left time for family, friends and writing
the stories she really wants to tell.

Other Silhouette Books by Kathleen Eagle

Silhouette Special Edition

Someday Soon
A Class Act
Georgia Nights
Something Worth Keeping

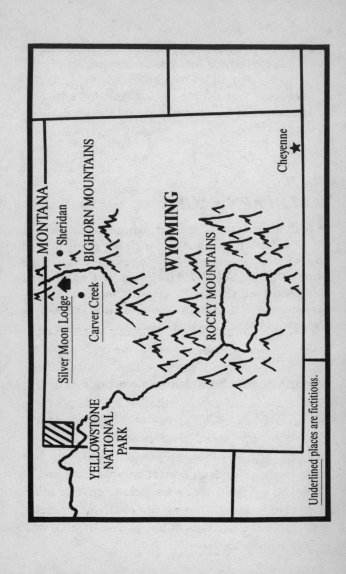

MONTANA

Silver Moon Lodge

Sheridan

BIGHORN MOUNTAINS

Carver Creek

YELLOWSTONE
NATIONAL
PARK

WYOMING

ROCKY MOUNTAINS

Cheyenne

Underlined places are fictitious.

Chapter One

Sky Hunter drank his tonic without gin. He liked it better that way. If he was working, the scene would be much the same as it was now—dark, smoky, a dull rumble of voices and a short, fat bartender behind a long, wet wooden bar. But then he would order gin and be served a glass of water. A week ago he had been Luke White Earth, and his demand for whiskey had been met with an ominous order to "clear out" because "we don't want no more trouble from you." He'd done a magnificent dark scowl and growled some threats before a magnanimous white man had emerged from the crowd and bought him a glass of what was really colored water.

As Sky Hunter, he would have had no trouble getting served liquor at Shorty's Bar, but he ordered his usual tonic with a twist of lime anyway. He thanked Shorty when the drink was set in front of him, offering a smile that Luke White Earth could not have managed. The polite amenities and the pleasant smile had become part of "the usual" for Sky, but as he looked around the bar, absorbing its familiarity, he remembered a time before Luke White Earth, even before Sky Hunter, when none of that was so.

He remembered being sixteen and being singled out from a group of cocky buddies seated at the corner table. Shorty had known somehow that Sky was younger than the rest, and he'd made Sky feel like the kid who'd been ordered to bed early. He'd been thrown out on his ear again three years later, when he'd gotten drunk and thrown a punch at one of the same good buddies. He'd missed his mark, but managed to break a phony antler off Shorty's prize "jackalope." He noticed that the stuffed rabbit's head was still missing a horn.

He'd been thrown out of classier places than this one in his early Hollywood days, but he'd never felt more humiliated than he had when he was sixteen. Then, nothing had been more important than hanging out with cowboys, but times had changed, Sky thought. He himself had surely changed. He'd hung out with the cowboys, and then he'd hung out with the people who'd created the image of the cowboy and the illusion of the Indian. He'd learned some hard lessons, and he'd changed his "usual." Tonic water with a twist. He'd had all the Hollywood highs he wanted, certainly more than he needed, and he knew for a fact that the only good high was a Rocky Mountain high. He'd come home for a taste of it.

The woman didn't catch his eye until she turned in her seat to call Shorty back, probably to change her order. Sky had been aware of the back of her blond head, but he had dismissed it, along with the rest of what was unfamiliar in the bar. He was here to reminisce, not to check out women. But when the blonde turned his way, he noticed, and so did she.

She didn't belong in a place like Shorty's, and she looked somewhat uncomfortable as she turned large blue eyes away from the stocky little bar owner and caught Sky staring at her. He didn't mind being caught. It was his habit to let a woman know she was being appraised. The reaction he got when he first looked at a woman was part of what interested him. This one wasn't cunning or coy. She simply returned his interest in full, wide-eyed measure. Since she was alone, he took his tonic to her table.

It struck her first that he was handsome, then that he moved with an easy grace, then that he was an Indian. Interesting, Elaina thought. She'd created so many Indian characters that she would have expected the impressions to come in the reverse order. She must be a woman first and foremost after all, she thought. Handsomeness caught her attention first, and handsome he was. Tall and lithe, he wore his black hair longer than was fashionable, but its coarse thickness had obviously been carefully shaped by a professional's scissors. The easy curve of a full lower lip and a well-shaped upper one contrasted with his face's angular bone structure. It was an exotic face, and yet there was something oddly familiar about it. Elaina would have termed the Roman nose characteristic, but his eyes, almond-shaped and slightly hooded, were unexpectedly penetrating. They were liquid brown, almost glossy, and they spoke of his interest in her before he uttered a word.

"You must be new to these parts," he drawled with a hint of a smile. "You don't look quite as bored as the natives."

He stood by her table, drink in hand, and he drew a smile from her before she considered the risk in giving one. "How quaint! Do people in Wyoming really say, 'You must be new to these parts,' or is that just a conversation starter?"

"Invite me to sit down and I'll give you a pretty good idea of how people from Wyoming talk." He gave her a moment to consider. She wasn't sizing him up; he knew she'd already done that and not found him wanting by her standards, whatever those were. She was trying to decide how it would look for her to strike up a conversation so readily with a strange man, and she'd just about come to the conclusion that since she didn't know anybody here, it didn't matter. He set his drink down, waited for her to tilt her head in what could only be called a nonnegative response and then slid into the booth across from her. "If not me, it'll be somebody else."

"Oh, really?"

He had to hand it to her. She didn't get her back up easily. A little indignant, but he could take care of that. "These guys aren't going to let you sit here by yourself for very long. How many opening lines do you think you can stand?"

"One's enough. It's about all I have time for."

"Good. I'll sit here and fend off the rest. You're not meeting someone, are you?"

She glanced around as though checking. "Actually, I think someone *was* supposed to meet me here, but the bartender tells me no one's been looking for me yet."

His smile relieved the blackness of his eyes, which were too dark to allow anyone to see more than what he would deliberately show. "I could tell you I've been looking for you all my life, but I don't suppose you'd buy it."

"I don't suppose I could afford to." Shorty delivered her drink just then, and she noted that the man made no move to pay for it. She was glad not to have her assertiveness tested at that point. "I hope your conversation isn't just a bottomless pit of opening lines."

Shorty laughed as he plunked her change on the table. "Sky's real good with lines, ma'am. He oughta be. He's had years of practice."

"Then I'm obviously out of my league."

"I don't write 'em; I just say 'em." Sky braced his elbows on the edge of the table and leaned toward her, waiting for Shorty to waddle away. "If I sound like a walking cliché, blame the writers. They're all great cliché-makers."

"Really?"

"But then, it's not the words themselves that are important, is it? It's the...execution." He brought his glass halfway to his mouth before he added, "Or maybe the style."

Elaina studied his face again, that sense of familiarity tugging at her. "I've seen you somewhere before."

"Now there's a line I haven't heard before," he said sardonically.

This was the moment he always hated, and he didn't quite understand why. Yes, he was who she thought he was, and he made a damn good living at it. His name never meant much, but they always knew, after they'd looked at him for a while, that they'd seen him somewhere before. He sipped his tonic and let her realize...

"You're an actor, aren't you?"

Damn right, lady, good for you. "Yes, I am. Sky Hunter."

"Sky Hunter," she repeated slowly. "I don't believe I've seen that one. Was it out recently?"

Sky set his glass down, matching the bottom to the ring it had left on the table as he tried to think of an appropriately sarcastic response. He looked up, and the innocence in those blue eyes shot a hole in his sarcasm. He laughed. "Sky Hunter's no movie, honey, that's my name."

"Oh. I'm sorry." Sitting back in her seat, she laughed, too. "It's wonderful. It's . . . it's a whole image. Is it real?"

"Sort of. It is now, anyway. How about you? You have a name?"

"Elaina Delacourte."

"Wow. That's gorgeous." A teasing spark danced in his eyes. "Is it real?"

"Sort of. I'm one of those writers who comes up with all the clichés."

He laughed again, and she thought it made him look remarkably young. "God, that's good." When she only smiled, he gave her a puzzled look. "You're kidding, aren't you? You're not a screenwriter."

"I write novels. Popular fiction." In response to his raised eyebrows she added, "Romance."

He held his hands up in surrender. "Hey, as long as you're not a screenwriter, there was no offense intended."

"I wouldn't mind it," Elaina said, thinking of the people she knew who were trying to break into that field. "I hear it pays well."

"It shouldn't, not for ninety percent of them." He thought that over, the corners of his mouth turning down slightly as he lifted one shoulder and amended, "Maybe seventy percent."

"You're going to tell me they aren't writing scripts like they used to, right?"

"I'm going to tell you they aren't writing many good ones, and when they do..." Her blue eyes, bright with interest, stopped him cold. And when they do, what? he asked himself. There's never a part in it for you, but you're not going to tell this woman that. She's just met a movie star. Play the role. "When they do, it can be the makings of a great film. Just like a great book. Have you written a great book, Elaina?"

She straightened her shoulders and smiled. "I've written some very good books or so my readers tell me."

He was tempted to ask her what they knew, but he thought better of that, too. Readers were probably smarter than most moviegoers, anyway. "I guess I've been in some very good movies, too. People bought tickets to see them, so they must have been good." A taste of his tonic gave him a moment to change the subject. "Where are you from, Elaina Delacourte?"

"Minneapolis."

"Ah," he said, nodding. "Wholesome. So who's a nice girl like you supposed to meet in a sleazy place like this?"

Elaina glanced toward the bar. Shorty seemed to be keeping things clean, at least in that area; he was sponging up sloshed beer. The same whiny female singer was bemoaning her man's bad habits over the jukebox for the fourth time in a row. Elaina wondered if the machine was stuck on that song's number. "This isn't so bad. It's . . . quaint."

"I believe you used that word before." His teasing smile reached his eyes, and he accentuated the Western twang that, earlier, had been hardly noticeable in his speech. "My opener was 'quaint.' How about my accent? You like that, too? It's gen-u-ine cowboy and damned hard to unlearn."

"Damned hard to describe, too. Keep it coming so I can think of the words."

"This visit to Wyoming is in the interest of research, I take it."

Smiling, Elaina dipped her chin in acknowledgment. "Every time I leave the house it's for research. I'm taking a pack trip this time out. That's who I'm waiting for."

"What outfitter are you using?"

"Joe Two Moon," she reported. "Someone from Silver Moon Lodge was supposed to meet me here." She checked her watch. "Maybe I'm early. Do you know Mr. Two Moon?"

A grin split Sky's face, surprising Elaina with the intensity of its brightness. "Joe's the best. You'll have a good trip with him, I promise you, but he runs on Indian time." He nodded toward the jukebox. "We could probably take a few turns around the dance floor before he shows up."

"What dance floor?" The jukebox stood in a dark corner, but there was little space between it and the empty table nearby.

Sky was already sliding out of the booth and reaching for her hand. "The one we're going to improvise. I'm great at improvisation. I once took a course in it. Besides, we're due for a different song."

Sky was a good name for him, she thought, looking up as he stood by the table, waiting. He wore a pale blue Western shirt and jeans, very much in keeping with the dress code for Shorty's Bar, but he wore them with more style than Shorty's other patrons. The shirt's tapered cut flattered his shoulders, which seemed wider, and his torso, which seemed longer and leaner than everybody else's. In his profession there could be no little tire around the waistline, and the slender cut of his jeans was as important as the cut of a businessman's suit. Elaina took the hand he offered her and came to her feet, brushing at the wrinkles that would have fallen from her knit skirt without her help. "I thought maybe this was the bartender's favorite song."

"I think it's Tommy's favorite." Sky lifted his chin toward the end of the bar, where a man sat with his head in his hand and his nose in his beer. "He thinks that song was written about him. It probably was."

Sky shoved some change into the jukebox and pressed several buttons before he turned to Elaina. "The last choice is yours."

She'd paid no attention to his selections, but after a quick survey of titles, Elaina selected one. It surprised her when her choice came on first. Sky slipped his arm around her waist and pulled her close as Elvis's familiar voice crooned "I Can't Help Falling in Love with You." Only his right arm and his left hand actually made contact with her, but the scant space between their bodies quickly became heated, and Elaina felt as though she could draw only tiny breaths. He didn't move until she looked up at him, his eyes six inches above hers, and then he smiled and moved with the same grace with which he walked.

The song was a sentimental choice for Elaina. She'd loved Elvis's love songs since she was a child and had watched his movies on TV, donned her mother's cast-offs and danced around the living room. His voice always did funny things to her insides, just as it was doing now. Peering past Sky's shoulder, she realized she could have done without an audience. Shorty was standing behind the bar, grinning like a proud parent. At first, a dozen or more pairs of eyes peered through smoke and darkness to watch the spectacle, idle curiosity the only spark of life in some of them. Within a few moments the sparks dulled one by one, and the drinkers went back to their drinks, the boasters back to their boasts, the chatterers back to their chats. The monotonous din faded into the background, and Elaina heard only the music as four slow ballads played successively.

The scant space narrowed, and their bodies brushed against each other. Elaina's nerves tingled, and she lost track of what her feet were doing. She was starved for air, and she drew a slow, deep, shaky breath. His hand stirred at her waist.

"You've got nothing to worry about, Elaina," Sky said near her ear. "I'm a pussycat."

She lifted her head, frowning delicately. "I'm not worried."

"Some women are at this point."

"And just what is 'this point'?"

He smiled a slow, knowing smile. "The point where we test things out. We see how it feels to touch, using the socially approved method."

She had to remind herself that she knew all that. She *wrote* these scenes, after all. And it *worked*, by God, like a charm. His legs brushed against hers just enough to send a shimmering current of warmth from the point of contact to her stomach. She wondered whether the satisfaction she was feeling was predominantly intellectual or physical. Whatever it is, you're lost if you don't keep the conversation going somehow, she told herself. "Dancing?"

"Mmm. Right out here in front of Shorty and everyone. There's safety in numbers, and—" he took a deep breath "—your hair smells delicious."

Of course it did, she thought, that was part of the scene. And also, she'd just washed it with whipped coconut something. But that smell was supposed to be part of her. She wasn't supposed to say, "I just washed it."

He laid his cheek against the side of her head, and she could almost feel his mouth turn up in a smile. "It feels soft," he said. "I don't know what it is about women's hair. It doesn't matter what color it is, but if it's long and soft like this . . .''

"I feel silly dancing when no one else is," she said quickly.

He stopped and lowered his arms, looking down at her upturned face. "Then we'll sit down." The jukebox whirred and clicked, and "I Can't Help Falling in Love with You" began again. Neither of them moved until he took her in his arms for another dance.

"I didn't play this twice, did I?"

"No," he said as he tightened his hold on her waist and pulled her against him. "I chose it, too."

"You're an Elvis fan?"

"Mmm-hmm."

"Figures."

The music came to an abrupt end, and Sky and Elaina turned to find Tommy from the bar standing by the jukebox with the plug in his hand. "Enough of this garbage," he snapped. "This ain't no dance palace; it's a bar. I wanna hear 'Don't Come Home A-Drinkin' and 'I'm Gonna Hire a Wino to Decorate Our Home.' Good drinkin' music."

Sky moved away from Elaina, and with a glance and a reassuring gesture in Shorty's direction to let the bartender know his jackalope's other antler was safe, he reached for his wallet and pulled out a bill. Tommy didn't protest when Sky took the cord he'd been waving out of his hand.

"Tell you what, Tommy. You take this plug and shove it—" he nodded toward the empty outlet

"—back in that wall so the lady can hear the rest of her song, and I'll spring for 'Don't Come Home A-Drinkin' for the rest of the night." He offered both the cord and the cash. "Deal?"

Tommy glanced behind Sky and offered Elaina a smile as he accepted both offers. "I didn't realize this was the lady's choice. Sorry, ma'am." He touched the brim of his crumpled straw cowboy hat with the hand that was busy wadding the money. With a quick shove of the plug, he wound Elvis back up again. "Enjoy your dance." Elaina heard Tommy mumble, as he made his way toward the bar, "I would, too, if I had somebody to dance with."

Sky and Elaina took up where they'd left off, Elaina wondering how expensive this dance had been.

"You don't have a car here?" Sky asked after a little while.

"No. I flew to Billings and then took the bus."

"I'll take you out to Silver Moon," he offered. "Joe probably sent one of his boys after you, and the kid probably took a side trip to see a girlfriend." He smiled as a pleasant memory drifted by. "Don't tell on him, though. Joe'll have him mucking out stalls for a month."

"Is it far? I don't want to spoil your evening."

His dark eyes met hers, and this time they didn't tease. "You've made my evening unexpectedly pleasant, Elaina Delacourte. Shorty's is only good for a brief stop on my way through town, just to see how much has changed.'' He glanced behind her. ''And it hasn't changed a hell of a lot.''

'' 'You can't go home again'?''

"Oh, I guess you can," he decided, watching Tommy buy himself another drink. "But not to stay." The last strains of the song ended, and Sky held her for a moment longer. "Ready?"

Elaina nodded. He slid his arms away slowly, holding her with his hypnotic gaze. His gesture toward the door was the cue that released her. As she walked away from the dim corner and the jukebox, she felt a little disoriented, as though she was leaving a theater and facing a lobby full of people waiting for the next show.

Chapter Two

Something about the long silence and the looks Sky sent her way made Elaina uneasy. It was the kind of uneasiness she always felt before she went to a party or just before a thunderstorm—a delicious brand of dread. It was a forty-five-minute drive in Sky's sporty Camaro through country that seemed, in the darkness, like a moonscape, hilly and barren but for some indistinguishable brush that sped past the window. The Rocky Mountains loomed up ahead against a starry sky.

"I didn't realize it was so far," Elaina ventured, disturbing the silence. "I wouldn't have let you drive so far out of your way."

"No problem," Sky said, offering his passenger only a little piece of his attention. "It's just up the road here."

Elaina leaned forward and peered through the windshield, looking for some hint of light along the roadside. "What is?"

What is? his thought echoed. Where did you think we're... Ah, the lady was getting nervous, he realized, and since she didn't know him from Adam, he figured it was about time. "The lonely, deserted road." Each word was pronounced slowly and precisely in a hauntingly deep voice. "The one that leads to the lonely, deserted mountain."

"What?" Lonely and deserted described the road they were on right now. Surely it didn't get any more desolate than this. She risked a glance at him and noticed that he wasn't smiling.

Her small voice gave him a little thrill of guilt, and he had to remind himself to keep his eyes steadfastly on the road and not take a look at her face. "The lonely, deserted mountain, where I've already prepared the hole."

"What hole?" Oh, God, what was she doing in this car with this man?

"The one we'll bury you in up to your neck before we pour honey over your head and dance around you until the sun comes up."

Elaina stared at his stony profile, and her heart tripped over her esophagus on its way to her mouth. "Is this some kind of a joke?"

"Red ants are no joke, white lady. Not when your face is dripping with honey, and the sun is..." He couldn't resist taking that fatal look at her, and then he ruined it all with a chuckle. She looked scared. Served her right for accepting a ride with a stranger. "I forgot. You're not into Westerns. You write that romance stuff. You'd have me taking you up the lonely, deserted road and having my savage way with you, right?"

"No...no, of course not." He was kidding, obviously. He wasn't dangerous; she'd known that all along.

"No? Red ants or rape—it's gotta be one or the other, or we won't have much of a story here. Suppose you had a choice."

"Between red ants and a fate worse than death?" She settled back in the bucket seat, telling herself it was silly to feel relieved. It had been obvious the whole time that he was kidding. "Couldn't I have maple syrup with the ants instead of honey?"

He laughed. "We don't have any maple trees around here. Honey's all we've got to work with."

Elaina shrugged and offered a tentative smile. "I could bring my own syrup. Pure Minnesota maple."

"We've gotta read the script the way it's written, sweetheart." His eyes were bright now with his teasing, even in the near-darkness. "Don't want to offend the writers, do we?" Smiling, she shook her head. "Of course, if you choose the red ants over me, I'll be truly offended. Crushed, in fact."

"If I were writing this story, you might start out with rape in mind, but you wouldn't be able to go through with it. You'd see the terror in my eyes, and your conscience would shift into overdrive."

"Conscience?" He considered her face for a moment as though looking for that terror in her eyes, and then he turned his attention to the road. "You're going to give me an attack of conscience right now. And what in hell am I going to do with that when I've already got my hole dug?" Hearing it, Sky realized what a damn good question that was. Conscience was unnecessary baggage when he was already thinking about seeing her again.

"Ah, you're going to keep me pure and chaste so I can become your wife."

"But you can't marry a savage."

"I'll have to struggle with it for about three hundred pages, but it beats red ants or rape."

Sky gave a quick laugh. "If we're talking over a hundred years ago, you flatter yourself. I wouldn't have been as impressed with your pretty blue eyes as I am now. We used to think you guys were pretty sickly looking." Grinning, he broadened his drawl. "We couldn't stand the way you pilgrims smelled until one of you came up with deodorant." He tossed her a wink. "You've come a long way, baby. Oh, jeez—" With a quick glance past her, he frowned as he slowed the car. "I missed the turn."

"We passed the lodge?"

"No, we passed the lonely, deserted mountain. Here's the turn to the lodge." Elaina caught a glimpse of a sign as they turned onto a gravel road. "Just as well," he added. "You were about to opt for red ants anyway, weren't you?"

"I imagined both alternatives," Elaina said, thinking that she was glad he hadn't been able to see the visions in her mind.

"And?"

"And I was beginning to think there probably wouldn't be anything worse than having my face chewed up by a million ants."

Sky chuckled. "I probably wouldn't have had the stomach for it, either, no matter which fate you chose. Good thing I missed the turn."

"Good thing you found this one. These people must wonder what happened to me."

"Joe should've gone down to Shorty's himself," Sky muttered. This woman wasn't a pickup, and for some reason it bothered him that she'd gone with him so easily. Maybe it was *her* conscience that needed beefing up. He slowed for the wire gate he knew was stretched across the road just ahead.

"What's wrong?"

Sky opened the car door, explaining, "Gotta get the gate."

What was ahead didn't look like a gate to Elaina; it looked like a barbwire fence inconveniently positioned across an access road. She pushed aside her niggling worry over the fact that she had no idea where she was and watched Sky in the splash of light the headlights provided. He pulled the wire loop over the gatepost and peeled the four-strand barbwire gate across the road. Then he drove the car through and got out to close the gate behind them. When he got back in, he cocked a finger at her as he moved the car forward. "Ordinarily, that's the passenger's job, but tonight you got a break."

She cast a look over her shoulder at the darkness behind the car. Red ants or rape. "Tonight I needed a break," she mumbled.

He grinned at the rutted road ahead. True, he'd had a little fun at her expense. *Red ants or rape.* "Tonight I owed you."

In the dark the lodge looked like what she remembered of the Ponderosa from TV's *Bonanza*. It was a sprawling log structure surrounded by log railings and a big, rustic veranda. A single porch light burned. Sky retrieved Elaina's bag from the back of the car. She reached for it, and he handed it to her with no insistence that he carry it for her or see her to the door. He figured on making a clean getaway.

"Thank you for the ride."

"Thank you for the dance."

"Can I . . . pay you something?"

Pay me for what? The ride or the dance? He smiled pleasantly. "Struggling over the choice between me and the red ants was bad enough. Don't compound the insult by offering to pay me for being a gentleman."

She returned his smile. "I'm sorry. It was kind of you to drive me out this far."

"Out here, you have to give people a hand once in a while. You never know when you might be stuck for one yourself." He nodded toward the lodge's big front door. "Looks like they've all gone to bed, but the door's always open, and there's a bell on the front desk. If that doesn't do it, holler for Jenny. Old Joe sleeps like a log."

Elaina nodded. She was going in, and he was leaving. Her lightweight bag dangled from her hands as she bounced it against her knees. "It's been . . . really nice meeting you."

"Same here. Listen, do yourself a favor."

"What?"

"If you don't wanna look like such a dude, don't look so wide-eyed every time someone tells a whopper. You're gonna hear some incredible tales around those camp fires. Just remember that incredible means unbelievable."

Elaina laughed softly. "I'll remember."

He nodded his approval and walked around the car to the driver's side. She took a step back, still watching him, and he grinned at her over the roof of the car. "You know anything about riding a horse?" he wondered.

She shrugged. "Six lessons at fifteen dollars an hour. I should hope so."

He laughed and shook his head. "Remember to dismount on the high side of the trail. And take some liniment along—for yourself, not the horse."

"I expect to be a little sore the first day out."

"You won't be disappointed."

"I hope not." She looked toward the mountains, which seemed to hover like dark giants in the night. "It *is* beautiful up there, isn't it?"

He followed the direction of her gaze. "It sure is." He looked back at her, thinking, yes, you'll complement the scenery, Elaina Delacourte. "Have a good trip."

The car door slammed and he was gone, swallowed up quickly by the night. Elaina uttered a belated thank-you and mounted the lodge's wooden steps.

The big front desk was the only thing that identified the building as a lodge instead of a private home. Elaina glanced around, liking what she saw. Although the living room to the right and the dining room to the left could accommodate several families, the furniture was homey, and the colors, though they blended, didn't match perfectly. The place had been decorated by a family, not a corporation.

At the sound of the desk bell, there was a stirring at the top of the open pine stairs. Pink slippers and the bottom of a chenille housecoat came into view, followed by the body and then the round face of a woman with one long, dark braid hitched over her shoulder. She hesitated on the steps, giving Elaina a curious frown. "Can I help you?"

"Yes, I have a reservation. Elaina Delacourte. I'm taking a pack trip with you this week."

"Elaina Delacourte," the woman repeated, hurrying to the bottom of the steps. "You're the writer, aren't you? You wrote that in your letter, and I got one of your books." Jenny reached for the chain that dangled under the desk lamp and fished a pair of wire-rim glasses out of her robe pocket. "We were expecting you tomorrow. The pack trip leaves Sunday morning. How did you get here?"

"I flew to Billings and took the bus to Carver Creek," Elaina explained, setting her bag down in front of the desk. "I'm sure I had a reservation for tonight."

"I do have a room for you, but..." The woman flipped a page in the big brown register, scowling until she found a note. "Eeee, that's right. 'E. Delacourte. Meet guest at Shorty's, Friday, 7:00 p.m.,'" she read, pointing to the note. "It's right here, and I thought I knew when everyone was coming in, so I didn't even check. I bet you were waiting at Shorty's since... How did you even get out here?"

"Actually, I...met a friend, who gave me a ride."

The simple nod of acceptance surprised Elaina. She expected more questions, like who did she know in Carver Creek, but the woman only smiled and reached for Elaina's bag. "Good. It worked out for you, then. You must be tired after such a long trip. Let's go upstairs and find you a bed."

Elaina followed the woman, who introduced herself in a hushed voice as Jenny Two Moon, indicated the location of the women's bathroom and promised her a good breakfast at eight o'clock in the morning. "You have an east window," Jenny whispered. "The sun will wake you. And we'll find plenty for you to do with your extra day."

Elaina had planned the extra day so she could learn all she could about the outfitter's job and the preparations for the trip. She had hoped to get acquainted with her horse, as well. Jenny opened a door two down from the bathroom, flicked the light switch and indicated to Elaina that this spacious room, with its large, inviting bed, polished pine floor and heavy wood furniture, would be hers. Elaina expressed her thanks before Jenny closed the door behind her. Spreading her arms, Elaina flopped across the bed with a satisfied groan, noting that the room had no TV, no radio and that the only noise beyond the open window came from the crickets. What heaven!

Sky. Sky Hunter. He wasn't noisy, either. A softspoken man with a sense of humor and beautiful, dark brown eyes. Moments later Elaina crawled into bed and drifted to sleep, listening to the sound of the crickets, her mind filled with the memory of expressive eyes.

The early morning light woke her. She heard a pair of morning doves calling to each other across the yard, their voices a gentle announcement of the sun's appearance. The air in the bedroom was cool and crisp, and it made her skin tingle when she threw the covers back. The story that was taking shape in her mind would find more substance in this day's experiences, she knew.

She dressed in jeans and a cotton camp-style shirt, then struggled with her stiff new cowboy boots, tugging them over her high insteps. Checking herself out in the full-length mirror that hung on the door of an old-fashioned wardrobe, she adjusted the jeans, which had gotten tighter after just one washing, and turned first to one side, then the other, looking for seams and bulges. Maybe they weren't *too* tight, but they sure looked new. She hooked her thumbs in her belt loops, flexed her knees and walked bowlegged toward her image in the mirror. Within a couple of days this was the way people would be seeing her, she thought, grinning at the prospect. She'd probably be the only guest on the trip who actually wanted to experience saddle sores.

When Elaina reached the steps she sniffed the air and picked up her pace. Breakfast was her favorite meal of the day. The smell of bacon and coffee drew her past the dining room and into a large, airy kitchen. Jenny and a younger woman, who was heavily pregnant, were jockeying eggs and bacon in and out of several skillets, and a giant of a man was just coming through the back door.

"Good morning!" Jenny turned Elaina's way with a smile on her face and a platter of bacon in her hand, both of which Elaina found appealing. "Breakfast always brings the guests down and the men in before I can even stick my head out the door. This is Joe, and this is Carol, our daughter."

"I sure was red-faced this morning when Jenny told me you had to hitch a ride last night, ma'am," Joe confessed as he stretched his hand out to Elaina. Carol offered a shy nod and kept busy at the stove. "We had it in our heads everybody would be here by tonight and plum forgot you'd reserved a day early."

"It worked out fine, Mr. Two Moon. I got to see a little of Carver Creek and experience some of that Western atmosphere."

"Call me Joe," the big man said. "And there's no charge for the room for last night. I should have been there to meet you like I promised. What with all them roughnecks soakin' up the beer at Shorty's, I sure don't like leaving my guests to fend for themselves. For the ones that come by bus, I like to be right on the spot when the bus pulls in."

"You go get comfortable in there, Miss Dela-courte," Jenny ordered, waving a big slotted spoon in the direction of the dining room. "We advertise 'family-style,' and that's the way we serve everything up. You just make yourself at home. Coffee's ready."

Joe joined Elaina at one of the four tables. Soon there were several cowboys, Joe's sons Rick and Teddy, Carol's husband John and their two children, and finally Carol and Jenny to share the meal. Elaina learned that Joe was Lakota Sioux, that Jenny was Cheyenne and that their lodge had grown from a cabin they'd built many years before. Their business had been created around the three horses Jenny had brought to their marriage as a dowry. Joe seemed anxious to tell Elaina about every aspect of trail riding and packing, but he admitted that the boys did most of the guiding now, while he "followed the shade around the house."

"You can follow it right to the basement today," Jenny said. "The washer's leaking again."

"Thought I fixed that," Joe grumbled, squinting up at Jenny. "It's always something. If I didn't know better, I'd swear you had it fixed so I can't get off in the mountains no more. Got any more spuds?"

There was a chuckle from John Gray Bear, Joe's son-in-law, who was sitting at the end of the table. "Ain't a horse on the place can tote you up that mountain anyway, Joe. What Jenny's been fixin' is too much good food."

Joe gave a wheezy laugh and patted his ample belly. "Used to be able to eat anything I wanted and never gain an ounce. After a while I had to make a choice between riding and eating." He clapped a hand on Jenny's shoulder and gave it a little shake. "Didn't take me long to make up my mind, did it, Ma?"

"He still goes on some of the overnights," Jenny explained for Elaina's benefit as she handed her husband a platter of hash browns, "but not the full week trips. His asthma's got too bad lately. Rick, Teddy and John are our guides now."

Joe turned a dark-eyed smile Elaina's way, and something in the way his eyes danced as he talked made her wonder if they'd met before. "You come on out to the barn with me after we're done here, Miss Delacourte. I'll get you lined up with the right horse and give you some pointers. And then we'll take a short ride and talk packin'. So eat up." Having helped himself, Joe was dishing potatoes onto Elaina's plate. "How much? Little bit? Whole bunch?"

The seconds didn't stop coming until she spread her hand over her plate with a firm, "Enough!"

The day passed quickly as Elaina got acquainted with Ruby, the sorrel mare that would be hers for a week. She learned how to saddle the horse and how to dismount on the right side as well as the left. As she practiced she thought of Sky's advice about getting off on the high side of the trail. Joe showed her some of the other equipment that would be used on the trip— the pack saddles, lightweight tents and bedding, and the cooking gear. He got a little dreamy-eyed when he described the meals that would be cooked over the camp fires. After her lessons, Joe left Elaina alone with her mare while he oversaw the final preparations.

Supper at the lodge was wholesome and hearty, and there were more acquaintances to be made as the other guests arrived. By the time Elaina got a few moments alone on the big veranda, it was after nightfall. She sat at one end of a creaking porch swing and rocked it absently with the toe of one dangling foot, listening to the voices in the living room and the clatter of dishes being stacked in kitchen cupboards. She liked to be aware of the sounds that gave a setting its special mood. Here in the mountains there was peace, she realized. The sounds coming from the house were comforting in the face of the night's haunting quiet.

"Got room for another passenger?"

Elaina recognized Sky's voice. Sitting up a little straighter, she turned toward the end of the veranda and saw him outlined in the shadows. "Sure," she said. "I guess I owe you a ride."

"I guess you do. And you look lonesome, besides." Sky hoisted himself up to the porch on one long leg and swung the other over the railing. There was a cigarette at the corner of his mouth, which allowed him to offer her only half a smile.

"Not at all. I'm enjoying the evening and thinking about the trip tomorrow." She slid over on the cushioned seat to indicate that he should join her. His appearance was somehow not surprising. In a subtle way he'd been on her mind all day, much like a melody she couldn't quite shake. He leaned his backside against the railing as he took another pull on his cigarette. He wore a straw cowboy hat and jeans, and looked more like the driver of a Chevy pickup than a sleek Camaro. "What brings you back out here tonight? Run across another stranded guest?"

"Actually, I came out this afternoon looking for a job."

"Oh? Did you find one?"

"Easy. Good help's hard to find, especially good *cheap* help. Joe couldn't afford to turn me down."

"Really?" Since he'd made no move to join her, Elaina pushed her toe against the floor again. The chain squeaked above her head. "Just how cheap are you, Mr. Hunter?"

"Dirt cheap." He leaned toward her to confide, "I can be had for a song. Do you sing, Miss Delacourte?"

"Not even in the shower."

Sky grinned. "Well, Joe does, so he's got himself another guide. Teddy likes to take the shorter trips now that he's got a girlfriend in town, and John would just as soon stick close to home and keep his wife happy."

"So I get an actor instead of a guide this trip?"

"You'll get a compass and a real good map," he assured her. "You wanted adventure, didn't you? They've given me all the good lines: 'Follow me,' 'Don't look down' and 'I'll keep a lookout while you go behind the bushes.' "

"Catchy. Do I have any lines?"

"Of course. You get to say, 'That was a brave thing you did back there,' 'I need help' and . . ." His voice dropped to a low rumble. " 'Don't leave me alone tonight.' "

He was joking again, Elaina thought, and she realized she was pleased with the prospect of his joining what she'd come to think of as *her* trip. She smiled. "What happens when you get us lost?"

"I don't get us lost. There's a mutiny, and the usurper gets us lost—that'll be Conlin, the guy with the wife and kid. Then he begs me to take over again. I refuse until the newlyweds, the Davis couple, have a fight when she finds out he's really on the run from an embezzling rap. But we find out he's taking the heat for his brother, and I deliver her baby—"

"She's pregnant?"

"Not yet." He shrugged. "We're stranded up there all winter. Hell of an adventure."

"And all I get to say is, 'That was a brave thing you did' and 'I need help'?"

"And 'Don't leave me alone tonight.' That comes after the bear attack." He finished his cigarette with relish, stubbed it out, then made a point of crumbling the butt and stashing the evidence under the porch. "That's my last cigarette for the summer." The declaration was made for his own benefit, but the explanation was for hers. "Joe's fired me more than once for smoking out on the trail."

"You mean you've failed at this job before?"

Chuckling, Sky joined Elaina on the swing. He sat right in the middle, leaving little space between them, and rested both arms on the back. "I've been fired from it more times than I can count, but I always get hired back. Must be my charm." He flashed her a white-toothed grin. "Or the fact that Joe's my uncle. My mother's brother. By Indian standards, that's a man's closest relative. I can always count on Uncle Joe when I need a job."

"And you need a job now?" she asked gently.

He pointed toward the mountains with his chin. "I need to be up there for a while."

"Why not go up by yourself?"

"I thought it might be more fun to go with you." The light in his eyes warmed his smile. "You've never been packing before, you don't know a damn thing about horses and you're a city dude."

"I'm being typecast."

He shook his head. "You're looking forward to this with all the excitement of a kid at Christmas, and I want to watch you open your presents. I'm counting on you to be awed."

"And awkward, ignorant and tender-footed."

"And funny." She smiled at him, and he felt his stomach tighten. How long had it been since he'd known that feeling? He couldn't remember. Dipping his head closer to her ear, he added quietly, "And natural. And so damn pretty it makes my throat go dry."

"Good line, Mr. Hunter." She managed a light tone of voice, but she wanted to believe that his throat *was* dry and that his insides fluttered just the way hers did.

"Thanks. Far as I know, it's original."

"Then I'll make a note of it. You may see yourself as my next hero."

The light from the window behind her made a halo around her golden hair. He tipped his head back to get a different perspective as he answered almost absently, "I don't think I'd mind being your next hero."

"In my next *book*."

"Whatever." He was losing touch with the sense of the conversation, reaching up to touch the softly curling ends of her hair. He had a fantasy that he was trapping light between his fingers.

Elaina's breath caught in her chest for just a moment. He wasn't really touching her, and yet he was, and there was a kind of wonder in his eyes. He could have been the child he'd mentioned, fascinated by the way the wrapping on his Christmas present shone in the light. Elaina was desperate for something to say. "You've worked here before as a guide, then."

"From the time I was about fourteen. And after I got out of the army, and even after I got into acting, I'd come here when times were lean . . . or when the world was too much with me, as the saying goes." He drew his hand back and smiled, setting the reverie aside. "So what you get on this trip is not an actor, Miss Delacourte, but the best guide Silver Moon has ever had. Joe's kids haven't been at it long, and John's heart isn't in it anymore. I'll give you your money's worth."

"Guaranteed?"

"Or your money back." She was pushing the swing in a slow, easy motion, and he glanced down at her foot, which provided the impetus. "New boots?"

"Yes," she said, looking down at them, too.

"You are going to be tender-footed."

"It was either new boots or old tennis shoes," she told him. "These are quite comfortable, actually."

"We're going to break you in right, ma'am. You and your new boots."

He was pleased with his promise, and it showed in the smile that played around his mouth and danced in his eyes. Elaina was pleased, too. The pack trip was meant to be an education for her, a change of pace. The blood coursing full-tilt through her system drummed another promise in her head. This man with the dark, smiling eyes would bring a change of pace from the lackluster eyes she'd turned away from lately. Like the prospect of scaling the Rockies, this man was exciting.

Chapter Three

O'Malley loved the open road, but the hairpin curves and switchbacks that lay among the peaks of the Wyoming Rockies had begun to wear on his stomach as well as his nerves. Tooling along a nice straightaway in his own Porsche was one thing, but negotiating the outer curve of a narrow two-lane in a rented Chevette was something else. O'Malley didn't like heights, and he didn't like narrow roads. Put the two together, and it made him downright uncomfortable. He didn't know why the agency didn't just forget about that damned Indian.

The reason, he realized, was that Sky Hunter made good money for them. Whenever a script called for an Indian, Marcus and Leed had the boy for it. Gen-u-ine

Sioux. Hollywood was becoming more conscientious about using real Indians in those roles, but Indian actors were few and far between. *Good* ones, anyway, like Hunter. The boy could act. Unfortunately, he was chomping at the bit for meaty parts. Did he want to play Hamlet, for God's sake? O'Malley clamped his cigarette in the corner of his mouth and grinned as he turned the wheel to follow another curve. Othello, maybe, he told himself. The dusky Moor. So okay, Hunter would probably do a hell of a job with a part like that, but it wasn't being offered unless he wanted to do summer stock. O'Malley discouraged summer stock when there were good, paying movie parts to be had. And he had a contract for one with Sky Hunter's name on it right in his breast pocket.

If he could get a signature, he'd secure a package deal for Marcus and Leed, and his employers would soon forget the little faux pas he'd made about actress Nancy Charles's plastic surgery. This little trek was the price he had to pay for losing the agency a good client. Pinnacle Productions wanted Hunter for two low-budget projects, and Marcus and Leed had its eye on a major piece of work for one of its big-bucks clients. It was a package that could make a lot of people happy—if Sky Hunter would come down off his artistic high horse.

Anyway, O'Malley told himself, Hunter wouldn't be a draw for summer theater. He was a memorable face without a name. He had a comfortable niche in the business, and O'Malley had helped him carve it out.

Not everybody could be a Redford or a Newman, and not every film could be an Oscar winner. Hunter was getting steady work, damn *good* work, O'Malley told himself, and he should be grateful.

Sure, there were some "four-wallers," wilderness adventure films for which the "four walls" of small theaters across the country were rented by the distributor, a reversal of the usual method of renting the films to the theaters. Sky particularly disdained those parts, but, what with TV and video, there was good money in them. And four-wallers were big on Indians. The boy had a damn good future, if he'd only lower his sights a notch.

O'Malley wanted Sky's signature on this contract. After that, the boy could take a couple of weeks to do his thing up here in God's country. Squinting into the morning sun, O'Malley flipped the visor down and smiled again. The Great Spirit's country, he amended. Whatever. He'd given up trying to figure anybody who wasn't Irish a long time ago. Everybody else had so many ethnic quirks, you had to carry around a textbook to keep up with them all. O'Malley liked to keep it simple, and he knew that no matter who he was dealing with, the bottom line was money. And there was enough tied up in this deal to make it worth the agency's while to fly him out to Billings, Montana, of all places, rent him a car and have him hand-deliver the offer.

Sky saw O'Malley coming even before the man parked his rental car at the end of a row of pick-ups. The agent was in a determined mood, and his too-sincere smile, which flashed the moment he emerged and stretched his legs, was the first signal. Sky paused to watch Carla and Mark Davis, the honeymooners, as they tried out the pair of palominos he'd just helped them select for the pack trip. He decided to give O'Malley about five minutes to say his piece.

"What glorious country this is, Sky. Glorious! Such scenery!"

O'Malley always offered a handshake with his palm down and always grabbed a man's forearm with his other hand. Sky turned away from the couple and allowed his hand to be pumped. "Hello, O'Malley."

"Surprised to see me, are you, boy?"

O'Malley wasn't more than ten years Sky's senior, but Sky was always his "boy." And O'Malley was always O'Malley. "I'm never surprised to see you. You pop up anywhere and everywhere."

O'Malley's laugh, as always, seemed to be a natural and unrestrained response. "I swear, I didn't know you weren't alone in the Jacuzzi that time. I never interrupt a man when he's pursuing his pleasures."

"Good. I'm about to have the pleasure of a shower before I head out to where there aren't any." Sky gestured toward the lodge's front door. "Jenny's probably got a room for you, if you can do without room service and bellmen. The rooms are clean, and the food's great."

O'Malley fell into step beside Sky as he headed for the porch. "I'd enjoy it, Sky, but I really should get back. I brought this contract out because we're working with a deadline here, and I promised to deliver you by August one."

"The Pinnacle Productions deal?" Sky's boot hit the first step.

"Right. They've sweetened it."

"Not interested."

"What do you mean, you're not interested?" O'Malley caught the screen door behind Sky and followed him from the bright sunlight into the dark interior. "You haven't heard it yet."

"Don't have to. I read the script." Jenny stood near the front desk, and Elaina was just coming down the stairs. Sky's attention flitted from one to the other, resting for a moment on Elaina. Dressed in jeans and a bright golden yellow long-sleeved shirt, she looked like morning, the best part of the day. Her blond hair was caught up from her temples with a long barrette, and she smiled when she saw him.

"Ladies, this is O'Malley, my agent," Sky announced, reluctantly shifting his eyes to Jenny. "My aunt Jenny and Elaina Delacourte, an...adventuress."

"Adventuress?" O'Malley's voice skittered over the word like lard on a hot griddle. "How charming. And, Jenny, you have a lovely place here. Breathtaking."

"O'Malley is here to harass me, but since I'm cuttin' out this morning, I don't know whether he wants a room or not." He arched an eyebrow at the agent.

"What about it, O'Malley? Your blood pressure might come down a notch if you take it easy for twenty-four hours."

O'Malley glanced around, nodding with apparent approval. "I used to go to summer camp when I was a kid. Same camp every summer. Swimming, canoeing, horseback riding. The main building looked a lot like this."

"Stay overnight and reminisce, then," Sky suggested, heading for the stairway. "I want to grab a quick shower before—"

"Look, Sky, sign the contract," O'Malley pleaded, pulling the paper from the pocket of his sport coat. "Read it, sign it and we'll both enjoy our wilderness weekend more." He pushed the contract toward Sky's chest. "The money's good, Sky, and the terms are—"

"Tell them to get me a decent part, O'Malley."

"The terms are excellent."

"I don't need excellent terms on a lemon."

"It's a lead."

"The script stinks."

The two men stood head to head, Sky topping O'Malley by several inches. "I told them I'd deliver you. They've been more than generous because they can't feature anyone else in this role." There was a moment's silence. "There's a sequel in it for you." More silence. "What'll it be, Sky?"

"A shower." Turning on his heel, Sky stalked past the two women and headed upstairs.

"Bullheaded, stubborn..." Bracing one arm on the front desk, O'Malley cocked the other at his hip, shaking his head. "He's cutting his throat. Every time I give that boy a little slack, he wraps it around his neck. You a friend of his, Elaina?" Elaina was allowed just enough time to crease her brow and open her mouth. "Of course you are. His eyes fairly popped out of his head when you came down the stairs. *You* tell him. He thinks he can set the town on fire with his talent if he gets the right part. *You* tell him; he won't listen to me. That town doesn't ignite so easily. All he's burning is his bridges."

"He's taking a shower," Elaina said with a shrug. "Maybe that'll cool things down a little."

"Have you had your breakfast, Mr. O'Malley?" Jenny asked. "You must have been on the road before sunup."

"Yeah, well ... I flew in last night, thought I could handle this in a day's time. I guess I could use a good meal."

"And probably a good night's rest." Jenny motioned O'Malley toward the dining room. "People from Hollywood always need rest."

Elaina watched O'Malley retreat to the dining room with Jenny, who seated him near the kitchen door and appeared to listen to him as he continued to bewail Sky's stubbornness. O'Malley was obviously a persistent man, and Elaina wondered how a business relationship between persistence and stubbornness fared. She glanced up the stairs, in the direction Sky had taken, and wondered which one would get his way.

Rick Two Moon checked the rigging on his string of five packhorses. Each horse carried a set of canvas and box panniers that hung over a "sawbucks" atop the animal's back and held about 150 pounds of camping gear and supplies. Four tents were required for this party—one for the honeymooners, one for the family of three, one for the guides and one for Elaina—and all were lightweight, made especially for hikers and packers. The cooking gear, except for three Dutch ovens, was chosen for minimum weight, maximum efficiency. Succulent meals made in the Dutch ovens had given Silver Moon its reputation for providing good food on the trail. Nonperishable food and some frozen perishables were packed, but fresh supplies would be delivered to the party at given pickup points as they were needed.

Elaina was as interested in learning the technical aspects of packing as she was in enjoying the scenery, and she watched the final preparations carefully. Her horse, Ruby, carried a pack behind the saddle in which Elaina had stowed her own personal items—clothes, toiletries, camera and notebooks. The pack also contained her tightly rolled lightweight sleeping bag and a thin foam sleeping pad. Carrying her supplies was her only responsibility. Joe had assured the group several times that the guides would take care of everything else. That sounded fine, except that Elaina was

anxious to learn, and she watched with the idea of offering to help once the trip was under way.

Guarded glances at Sky told her that this was not
the time to offer her services. If he'd been away from
horses for any time at all, it didn't show. He helped
each guest to saddle up, checking cinches and stirrup
lengths, and finally swung onto his own horse, having expended little energy and few words. He was satisfied to leave all unnecessary noise, including
O'Malley's, behind him.

Leading the string of pack horses was Rick's job,
and he made the task look easy. It was a job Sky had
never liked, because it made him feel tied down. He
preferred to ride out front, leading the way into the
back country. There was peace there. Decisions came
easily. You took the trail down to the lake or the one
to the overlook, or you found your own. You just did
what felt right. And, as Sky remembered, it was wonderful to do what felt right. He wanted to make his
own choices, and he wanted to get out front and lead
the way.

"I understand you're quite a fisherman," Elaina
said, breaking his concentration. He raised an eyebrow as he looked back at her over his shoulder, and
she cleared her throat and smiled. "Your uncle told
me. He said you'd probably provide some of our best
meals when we got to the lake."

Sky glanced back at the rest of the group, which
followed in a cluster of three, then two, then one. With
a pair of honeymooners and a family on vacation, Sky

decided that he and Elaina were already a couple, in a way. Rick was an excellent wrangler, but not much of a conversationalist, unless he was telling tales by the fire. Sky figured it would be him and Elaina, and he figured she figured it, too. His smile moved slowly from his eyes to his mouth, welcoming her to the front of the line. "Do you like pan-fried trout?"

"I don't think I've had much fried fish, but it sounds great." Leather squeaked as she turned in her saddle. "I thought...I mean, I've *read* that the Sioux never liked fish much."

"Did I tell you I was Sioux?" He didn't remember. This was Shoshone, Crow and Northern Cheyenne territory, but most non-Indians didn't bother to notice that an Indian wasn't just an Indian.

"No, but your uncle is, so I assumed..."

"You're right. I like fish, though." He frowned, appearing to give this problem some thought. "Maybe I'm not really Sioux. Maybe the nurses switched babies on us at the hospital, and I'm really Flathead or Blackfoot. Do they like fish?"

"I don't know." Elaina frowned right along with him, trying to remember whether her research had turned up any facts on Flatheads and fish.

"Should we head north and find out?" He met her creased brow with a nod in that direction. "They live in Montana, and they've got lots of fish up there. Hell, I've gotta find out where I get this penchant for fish. You know, I haven't once craved any dog meat, and the Sioux were dog eaters."

"Well, I don't think...they don't eat dog *anymore*, do they?"

"I don't know. Do they?" He shrugged innocently. "Like I said, I'm a natural-born fish eater myself." Reaching under his denim jacket, he pulled out a paperback book with a familiar red-and-gold foil cover, which Elaina recognized as the popular historical novel she'd published several months before. "Pretty interesting reading, and I'm only on page seventy. This poor lady's in for some problems. Her *captor* is liable to devour her lapdog as well as her innocence."

Elaina eyed the book, feeling a little uncomfortable at the sight of it in Sky's hand. "The dog runs away," she told him quietly.

"Just disappears?" She nodded. "How can you be sure ol' Fast Horse didn't eat him?"

"Because I wrote the book, and *Swift* Horse wouldn't do that."

Leaning back in the saddle, Sky gave her a grin. "The hell he wouldn't. He's gotta eat something if he won't eat fish."

"Buffalo."

"Oh, yeah, buffalo. I understand you have to acquire a taste for it, sort of like—"

"Dog," she finished for him. "You don't like the book."

"I'm only on page seventy." He tucked the book back under his jacket. "Jenny wanted me to get you to sign it for her, but I thought I'd read it first."

"I did a lot of research for that book." It was true, but she knew it was foolish to feel so defensive about it.

"Sold the movie rights yet?"

"I doubt that it'll—"

"Do your own screenwriting," he advised. "Your dialogue is pretty good, but they'll butcher it."

Elaina brightened. "You like the dialogue? I worked hard to keep it from being wooden."

"As in 'cigar store'?" he injected.

It sounded like a comment that might have some teeth in it somewhere, and it bothered her. She'd wanted the compliment to stand. "Wooden as in stiff. I try to make my people talk like people, not caricatures. *All* my people."

"Your people?" He fixed his gaze on the slope ahead, where pines marched row on row, their ranks thinning toward the top. "You write people, and I do characters."

"Most people would say I write characters, too, but I think of them as people. They have to be alive for me, but I don't think I have to become them the way you do. I just have to know them...intimately."

"Intimately?" He turned a testing smile on her. "How many Indian men do you know...*intimately*?"

She swallowed, but stood her ground. "I know Swift Horse."

"Swift Horse is all pulp and ink. He's only Indian because you say he is." He scanned her face for a moment, the smile gone now from his. "Maybe you need to expand your research a little."

"I am," she said. "I'm observing you."

His look was dark for a moment, but a slow smile improved it. "Then I'll do my very best Sky Hunter while I return the compliment."

It was the practice to make camp early at the beginning of the trip. Those first hours in the saddle grew long, and Elaina was glad to make contact with the ground, even though she failed to manage the graceful dismount she'd been taught. The bones below her waist had apparently liquified. Rick and Sky unloaded the pack horses, while each guest unsaddled his own mount. Rick knew which horses would be likely to stray, and those were hobbled in a grassy dell nearby. The rest were released in the company of a mare, who had a tinkling bell around her neck to signal their whereabouts.

Rick got supper going in his trio of Dutch ovens, while Sky helped the guests acquaint themselves with their accommodations. The tents were easy to manage, and the bedrolls with their foam pads weren't uncomfortable, if a gravel-free site could be found.

"What's your name?" Sky asked the Conlins' twelve-year-old towhead. He'd introduced himself to the boy's parents before they left Silver Moon, but the kid had gotten left out somehow. Sky remembered being twelve years old and being just as invisible to adults.

"Danny."

"That's a good name." Sky offered the boy a handshake. "My name's Sky, but I sure like the name Danny. It feels friendly when you say it, don't you think?" Danny grinned and nodded. "I noticed how well you handled that horse. Have you done much riding?"

"No, not much."

"You like horses, though, don't you?" Danny nodded vigorously. "I can tell. You're a natural. You like to..." A branch cracked somewhere in the distance, diverting Sky's attention in that direction. In a moment two horsemen emerged from the trees. It was John Gray Bear, Rick's brother-in-law, and, damn his hide, it was O'Malley.

"What the hell are you doing here?"

O'Malley grinned down at Sky. "It's been a lot of years since summer camp, my friend, and I'm not sure I can get down off this beast without disgracing myself. What do you suggest?"

"I suggest you go back the way you came and get off in front of the lodge. What are you trying to prove?" Not interested in an answer, Sky fired his next question at John. "Why did you bring him up here?"

John shrugged. "He paid me to."

"When I went to Hawaii I tried surfing," O'Malley volunteered. "I tried cricket last time I went to England. So here I am in Wyoming. Now, how do I get down from here without landing on my butt?"

"I'll give you a hand, Mr. O'Malley," John offered, swinging down from his own mount.

Sky put his hands at his hips and gave a quick sigh. "I needed this trip, O'Malley."

"I need this deal, Sky, but I'm not here to pressure you. I really didn't want to pass up this once-in-a-lifetime—" O'Malley's knees gave way when he hit the ground, but John was there to steady him "—opportunity. Joe tells me I'm in for some fine cuisine." The word Sky muttered brought a look of mock distaste to O'Malley's face. "I was promised better fare than that."

"That's what you're gonna be scraping off your three-hundred-dollar shoes every night, O'Malley. This ain't your style."

John led the horses away, and O'Malley made no overtures toward helping him unload. Instead he followed Sky. "My style is persistence."

"I know."

"Once you sign, I'll have John take me back. After supper, that is. Then everybody's happy, and nobody gets anything on his shoes."

"Too late, O'Malley." Sky picked a stick up off the ground and handed it to O'Malley without any hesitation. "Don't come to supper without cleaning yourself up first."

Supper was everything that had been promised. Rick's Dutch ovens brought forth ham and new potatoes, biscuits and cherry cobbler. Seated on logs, the group made a congenial circle around the camp fire and raved about the food. The sincerity of the compliments was borne out by the number of seconds—

and thirds—that were served. By the time the spoon scraped the bottom of the last pot, most of the guests had slid to the ground, sprawling with their backs against the logs, their bellies too full to move. John and O'Malley had their cigarettes by the camp fire. This was the only time the ban on smoking was lifted, this easy, comfortable time around the fire. It was time for storytelling, and maybe for some music, if the guests were willing.

"When we get up in the high country tomorrow, you people keep your heads up and your ears cocked," Rick warned quietly. Arms braced on his knees, he cradled a cup of coffee in both hands and peered into it for inspiration. "The trail gets narrow, and there's falling rocks sometimes. You gotta watch out. Right, Sky?"

"Right."

Rick frowned at his coffee. *Right?* Maybe Sky had forgotten this part of his job, or maybe Rick hadn't offered the right cue. He'd try again. "'Course, sometimes it's more than just a little falling rock, right, Sky?"

"Sometimes."

Rick glanced up at Sky and found him staring into his coffee cup, lost in his own world. The story had been Joe's and Sky's, and they'd done it with the timing of a vaudeville team and the deadpan expressions of the best low-key humorists. As a boy, Rick had loved his father's stories, but they were never so animated as they could be when Sky, the natural actor, took part.

"Think we might stir up a real slide?" Rick persisted.

"Might."

"Not like the one Mrs. Bigbody got started when we was up here a few years back," John contributed, and Rick cast his brother-in-law a grateful glance. "You and me was just learning the ropes, but Sky was...you remember that one, Sky? Mrs. Bigbody?"

"Yeah. She was something else."

Sky had missed too many cues, so it was up to Rick and John to carry the story. Throwing the outrageous details back and forth and embellishing them with broad gestures, they had the group chuckling over the description of Mrs. Bigbody, for whom Joe had procured a Clydesdale for the trip into the high country. Mr. Bigbody was a runt whom the missis kept on a short leash. If he strayed from her sight, she yodeled for him like an Opry star. The story had it that her yodel brought half the mountain tumbling down on top of them, with Joe sprouting wings, Sky performing his first movie stunt and Mrs. Bigbody riding a huge boulder to the bottom of the canyon, yodeling all the way. The runt had vanished, but legend said that he was up there in the mountains somewhere, listening for that yodel, and if he heard it or anything that sounded like it, "you'd better look out below."

The story brought a smile to Sky's face, but he passed on the cue for the next one, as well. Elaina was enjoying herself, and he concentrated on her delicate laughter, letting it soothe him as he tried to ignore O'Malley's presence. The man was the classic pusher, and Sky bowed his neck until it ached from the stubborn resistance when he felt he was being pushed. O'Malley stood to gain more from this deal than a part for Sky, or he wouldn't have gone to all this trouble. O'Malley was playing a game, and Sky couldn't see the whole board, but he sure as hell wasn't anybody's pawn. Not anymore.

Uncurling himself, Sky rubbed the back of his neck and poured the remains of his coffee on the ground behind him. He wanted out. "You folks enjoy the camp fire," he said, stepping over a log. "But remember, 5:00 a.m. comes pretty early."

There was gear to be organized, horses to be tended and food was suspended out of bears' reach on lines strung between trees. Sky busied himself apart from the group, angry with O'Malley for spoiling his evening, angry with himself for letting him. When the storytelling was over and the guests started wandering toward their tents, O'Malley sought a few more words with Sky.

"Nice night."

"Yeah."

"Smell that air."

Silence.

"That's real pine, isn't it? Smells better than that plastic thing sitting on the top of the commode."

"Humph."

"Gets chilly when the sun goes down."

Silence.

"I must be addicted to smog. My lungs are crying for a little more substance." He patted the pocket where his cigarettes were kept, but he caught Sky's warning glance and let his hand drop.

"You know where to find it," Sky said grimly.

"And you know where to sign. All I need's a name, boy."

The last word was a dart, and it landed squarely on Sky's most sensitive nerve. He wasn't anybody's boy. One knot secured the end of a rope to the limb of a tree. He'd been careful to protect the tree with a piece of burlap, but he'd done nothing to protect himself from the knot forming in his own stomach. He turned slowly and took a deep breath.

"Seems to me I've heard that line before, or some version of it. Something like: 'You're a hell of an actor, boy. All you need's a name.'"

"And you've got one, Sky. Didn't we make a name for you? You've got work." The white paper O'Malley pulled from his pocket seemed luminous in the dark. "Right here. There are a lot of actors who can't get work these days but you've got it. You're in demand for the kind of role you do best. Take it, Sky. Take it and stay in the business. You turn this down—" O'Malley shook his head "—and you might not work for a good long time."

"I'm not interested in any more four-wallers with twenty lines of dialogue in the whole film. I don't want to do any more sidekicks or mean-faced drunks or sad-faced drunks or anybody with the nickname 'Chief.'"

O'Malley slapped the contract with the back of his hand. "This part has dignity, Sky. No lie, real dignity. It's sort of the dying race thing, but the character goes down fighting. He goes down—" the paper got another punch "—giving it all he's got. It's beautiful."

"Like hell. I told you, I read the script." Sky gave the knot one last unnecessary jerk. He'd already known it was secure. "Get me a part that doesn't call for an Indian."

"But you *are* an Indian. One of the few—"

"Yeah, one of the few. And I'm an actor. A good one, I'm told."

"One of the many vying for the few good parts. Being typecast isn't such a bad thing." O'Malley poked a finger toward Sky for emphasis. "A lot of people have made a damn good living being typecast."

"I can make a living guiding pack trips." Sky pushed the finger away from his chest and started walking toward the dying camp fire, tossing over his shoulder, "I want to act."

O'Malley followed, undaunted by Sky's rapid stride. "Just how far out of type do you expect to be able to get, Sky? I'm serious. I'm wondering what kind of work you expect me to find for you. I get you money, I get your name out, I get you respect...."

Sky whirled on his heel, his eyes glowing hot and angry. "I *earn* my money," he said quietly, aware of their proximity to Elaina's tent. "If there's any respect coming my way, I've earned that, too. Get me a part, O'Malley."

"What do you want to play?"

"A man."

Elaina emerged from her tent, and both men's heads turned. She looked at Sky, and he repeated quietly, "Just a man."

"I have to reach underneath and fish out all those little pebbles under my tent," Elaina told him as he came closer. She'd heard him arguing with O'Malley and thought he might appreciate the appearance of a third person. "I think John's looking for you, Mr. O'Malley. He wants to show you where the conveniences are."

"Looks like there's a whole mountain full of convenient trees," the agent said with a short laugh.

"Being civilized doesn't run very deep with you, does it, O'Malley?" Sky jerked his chin in the direction of the tent they'd erected for O'Malley and his guide. "You'd better let John teach you the finer points."

O'Malley glanced from Sky's face to Elaina's, then smiled. "I give you good-night, then, Miss Delacourte. And a highly civilized good evening to you, too, Mr. Hunter," he added with a mock tip of the hat before he turned and sauntered toward his tent.

Sky lowered one knee to the ground and reached for the nearest corner stake of Elaina's tent. "What are you doing?" she asked.

"It'll be easier to pull up stakes and move the tent than to try to reach under it."

"We don't have to do that. I can get along with the rocks better than you get along with your agent. I'll just ignore them."

He jerked the stake from the ground. "It's hard to ignore gravel when it's stuck in your craw. There's a nice grassy spot just over there."

Elaina glanced in the direction of his nod. "I saw that, but I thought we were making sort of a circle here." She indicated the arc of tents before she leaned down to tug on a stake.

"Then you should have known enough to face your door toward the east." He rose to his feet as she got the last stake. "You've researched the placement of a tepee, haven't you?"

"Of course, but I…" She ducked quickly inside the collapsing tent to gather her belongings. "Which direction was I facing?" she called out to him.

"Where does the sun set?"

Her bedroll emerged first, then her saddlebag and finally her saucy smile. "Behind the skyscrapers."

He laughed as he picked up the umbrella-shaped tent and moved it to the spot he'd selected. "Bring your stakes and one of your rocks. You might have to hit me over the head if I come tepee-creeping in the middle of the night."

They used the rock to pound the stakes back in, the tent door now facing east. Sitting side by side on the ground in front, they craned their necks to look at the stars.

"Nice night," he said, echoing O'Malley's observation. Funny, he thought. He'd forgotten O'Malley for a moment.

"Really is," she agreed. The air was cool, but it felt good. Maybe she'd put on too many layers; she felt a little warm.

"Did you get some good pictures today?"

"I think so. I almost got a pair of rabbits, but they ran away."

"We'll get you some big game," he promised, stretching one leg out in front of him. "So what kind of story are you writing that involves packing?"

"It's a contemporary romance with a little intrigue. The guide has an old grudge against the hero."

"The guide's the villain, huh?" He picked up a twig and tossed it into the night. "Where does the romance come in?"

"The heroine is the guide's sister."

"Figures. She's oblivious to his villainy."

"Of course. It's my first attempt at doing an Indian heroine. I think it's about time."

"So if they make a movie out of this, I could play the guide," he concluded.

"They've never sold movie rights to any of my books." Elaina stretched her legs out next to Sky's, but she failed to match his length. She sighed. "But wouldn't it be neat if they did? I'd love to go up to Winnipeg to one of those terrific fur shops and buy myself a full-length mink."

"You're too young for mink," he told her, tossing another twig. "How about coyote? How about you come back this fall and we go out and hunt you up a coyote coat?"

"I never thought of coyote."

"Sure. I could skin 'em out, and you could tan the hides and whip up a nice fur coat. You don't have to sell anything—no movie rights, no soul, nothing."

"What does Mr. Hunter get out of this?"

He shrugged in dismissal. "I get the thrill of the hunt. The adventure. The hours of stalking, the whang of the bow, the thunk of the arrow." She giggled, and he grinned. "I think I could write one of those myself. I've played so many of them, I..." He turned for a good look at her face. The moonlight and the distant, dying fire made her soft skin glow with a pale luminescence. "Wouldn't you like to live one of these crazy adventures? How would it feel if some of this stuff you write and I play really happened?"

"I don't know."

"Would it feel real?"

"I don't . . . know."

He caught her chin in the palm of his hand and gave her a soft kiss. His lips were moist, and the tip of his tongue greeted hers shyly. He pulled back half an inch, and Elaina drew a shaky breath. "It feels real," she whispered.

"It feels damn good. Like the beginning of an adventure." He kissed her again, his hand still cupped under her jaw. Elaina closed her eyes and savored the tingling in her own skin. But he drew away after the second kiss, and when she finally opened her eyes, the darkness was swallowing his form. "Good night, Elaina."

Chapter Four

The group slept quietly under a full white moon while Sky Hunter made his preparations. He sat on a log close to the firepit and thought about the crazy plan that had taken shape in his mind during the eerie quiet of the night. O'Malley had intruded, with John's help, and Sky had to get away. Sky had done John a favor by taking his place on this trip, but O'Malley's money had beckoned, and John had come along anyway. Fine, Sky decided. Now John owed Sky a favor. Sky was going to get his time away from Hollywood one way or another. The first way had been sane, but the second was a little crazy. As far as Sky was concerned, it was O'Malley's fault that he was leaning toward insanity. Hooray for Hollywood.

Sky rolled the log closer to the firepit and warmed himself at the remnant of the camp fire. He'd told Rick he would take care of the fire, and Rick had retired willingly. Rick worked hard helping his father run the trail rides and pack trips, and he deserved his rest. Sky would have enjoyed the week working with his cousin, but it just wasn't going to be possible. He wasn't going to spend a whole week in the mountains listening to O'Malley yap about that contract. He'd be tempted to sign it just to get the man off his back, and Sky wasn't going to let himself do that.

So they wanted him for another "noble savage" film. Much of the action would be slow-motion footage shot against a scenic mountain background, and most of the dialogue would make him sound like a stylized red man. They would pay him well to recreate an image that was as tired as Sky was and as unreal as he was beginning to feel. If he didn't accept that role, he'd be offered another token ethnic character in some cop movie. He wanted something else.

His gaze dropped from the treetops to a tent—the small nylon igloo that stood a short distance away. He wanted Elaina Delacourte, at the moment. There was nothing Hollywood about her. She was the main reason he'd offered Joe his services. Elaina was beautiful, and Sky liked the way she made him feel. He wasn't sure what to call the feeling; it was almost…softheartedness. Protectiveness, maybe. It had been a long time since he'd felt like protecting a woman. On the other hand, that romantic innocence was a nuisance, and he had a conflicting urge to shatter it. She'd come to this trip looking for a little adventure, and he figured she'd thrown some of her natural caution to the wind on his behalf already. Rising slowly to his feet, Sky decided that she was about ready to let the rest of it go the same way.

Her caution didn't fly immediately. When Elaina woke up enough to realize there was someone in her tent, Sky had to clamp a hand over her mouth to keep her from screaming. She relaxed a little when she recognized the voice whispering in her ear.

"Did you bring that rock to bed with you like I told you to?" he asked from where he was crouched behind her. Elaina nodded, the back of her head brushing against his jacket. "Can I count on you not to use it?" She shook her head vigorously. "How about if I promise no R and R?"

Muffled against his hand was a demand for clarification.

"No red ants and rape. Deal?" She nodded. "Whisper?" She nodded again, and he released her.

Scooting to sit up, she turned toward him, trying to make out his face in the dark. "What are you trying to do?"

"Shh." He touched his finger to her lips. "Whisper."

"Do you want to give me a heart attack?"

"If you don't keep your voice down I'll have to..."

"I thought you were going to..."

"...cut off your wind."

"... smother mmmmm ... mmm ..."

He kissed her hard until she kissed him back, and then he had to struggle to remember the detail of his plan, which didn't include making love to her right there and then. "Let's run away together," he suggested on the end of a sigh. He hadn't given the actual words much thought, and he was amazed that he was able to be so serious and sound so foolish.

"Sure. How about the mountains?"

"Exactly what I had in mind." She started to laugh, but he shushed her. "I don't want to stay with the group anymore. I can't deal with O'Malley. John brought him up here, so John can take my place. Come with me."

"Where?"

"Where they won't find us. Let me show you the mountains. Places nobody sees. Places worth writing about."

His voice was husky in the dark. Like blended whiskey, it was smooth and disarming, and he smelled of leather and woodsmoke, two scents that had always mingled in Elaina's mind to symbolize romance in the purest sense. She was gratified to find that they really did work that way. "I'm already seeing places worth writing about," she told him quietly.

"You're seeing a well-worn trail. You came for adventure, Elaina. I've got two saddle horses and one packhorse waiting to help you find it."

"Are you crazy? Just take off and ..."

"I don't know if I'm crazy," he said. His hushed tone was solemn. "If I am, the mountains can purge it out of me. I needed to come back. There was nothing else for me to do. And now..."

There was an edge in his voice that sounded almost like fear. It caught Elaina's heart and held it fast. "Would they follow us if we...if you just struck out on your own?"

"They'll probably try." He laid a hand on her shoulder. "It'll be fun giving John the slip, especially if O'Malley offers a reward for my capture."

A quick, low laugh bubbled deep in Elaina's throat. "I think I've already seen this flick."

"A hundred times," he assured her. "A hundred ways. Wanna try for a new angle?"

Her heartbeat thrummed in her ears. He was so close, and the tent was small, and his voice was rich and warm. She was still going on a pack trip, but she would have a private guide. She saw herself following him along a narrow mountain trail, and she knew she'd made her decision, though she wasn't certain when. "What's your angle?" she wondered, sliding out of her bedroll.

"I don't know yet. I'm making this up as I go along." She wasn't moving fast enough to suit him. He began rolling her bedroll, tugging at the corner she was kneeling on. If he kept her moving there was less chance she'd change her mind. "Is your saddlebag packed?" he asked as he tied up her bedroll.

"Pretty much. What are we going to eat?"

"I'll take care of that. You just get your boots on." She wasn't moving. "Ready when you are," he prompted.

"I'm not going like *this*."

"Why? What are you wearing?"

There was a pause. "Pajamas."

Another pause. "Oh. Sorry." Sky hoisted her bedroll over his shoulder and backed out of the tent, whispering, "You've got fifteen seconds to get into your riding clothes."

Elaina's pajamas were actually a set of long underwear. She was able to wriggle into her jeans and pull her boots on with about a second to spare. Ducking out of the tent with her jacket and saddlebag, she looked around quickly as Sky turned, his hands jammed in the back pockets of his jeans. He seemed surprised, as though none of this had been discussed and she'd just popped out of her tent in the middle of the night and found him there. They looked at each other for a moment before she thought to speak. He raised a finger to his lips, then nodded toward her tent. Wordlessly, they both knelt to ease the plastic stakes from the ground.

Elaina's mare wasn't one of the horses that had been hobbled for the night, so Sky had saddled the black gelding O'Malley had ridden for Elaina and a palomino for himself. A third horse would carry the panniers, which were ready, except for Elaina's tent. Elaina turned to watch Sky load the last horse with the packsaddle. "You must have been pretty sure I'd come."

"I hoped you would," he said, testing the weight of the loaded pannier. Experience told him the load was balanced. "I needed a tent. Mine wasn't empty."

"We could just tell them we're leaving."

He chuckled. "You don't tell anybody when you run away. Takes all the fun out of it."

"You don't think Rick will get in trouble with his father for losing a guest?"

"I'll be the one to get in trouble," he told her. "There'll be hell to pay when I get back, but I've been saving up for it." He concentrated on keeping the tension on his rope as he looped a modified basket hitch behind the panniers. He gave the knot a final tug and turned to Elaina, smiling. "I haven't done anything crazy in years. Life owes me a spree." Cupping a hand under her elbow, he directed her toward the saddle horses. "We'd better make tracks, honey, it's almost morning."

"Make tracks!" With her hand she stifled what threatened to be a hoot of laughter. "God, what awful dialogue."

He slid her saddlebag into place. "You like that, huh? There's more where that came from."

Groaning, she stuck her foot in the stirrup and levered herself into the saddle. Sky mounted, then led the packhorse, choosing their trail carefully in the darkness. Elaina followed, wide-eyed and wary. Every tree was a tall shadow, and every sound was the echo of something unknown. They passed by a small lake, where the moon made a long white trail on still, colorless water and two spectral deer drank their fill. As the sky lightened they made their way up a narrow trail to a grassy promontory, where they stopped for breakfast. Overhead, pink and blue streaks heralded the coming of the sun, and the air was still damp and chilly. They gathered a small bundle of wood and made a fire.

"How far have we come?" Elaina wondered out loud as she moved closer to the fire, and to Sky. He'd mixed up some biscuits and was frying bacon.

"Not more than a few miles. It's slow going in the dark."

"But we got away."

He looked up and saw the childlike satisfaction in her smile. "Yeah, we did. They'll be scratching their heads about now, wondering what the hell's going on."

"And sending someone out to look for us?"

"Probably. We'll let them see we're all right." He reached inside the box where he'd stashed his cooking supplies and came up with a small pan. "Coffee'll have to be instant. Can you boil water, Miss Delacourte?"

"The guests aren't supposed to have to work," she reminded him as she took the pan, "but I guess I'll make an exception."

"I'm revising the promotion a little. The guest doesn't have to work *too hard*."

Elaina measured water from the drinking pouch into the pan, which she brought and placed on the grate that Sky had laid over the small fire. "If we let them see us, won't they catch us?"

He heard a hint of worry in her voice, glanced up and caught the spark of concern in her blue eyes. She wanted it this way, he realized, and he smiled. "We won't let them catch us."

"I'd feel pretty stupid being caught for a runaway."

"You'd *look* pretty stupid. I can just hear your mother." He was busy forking bacon onto aluminum plates, which seemed appropriate, when he began to talk in a falsetto. "Elaina Marie, I don't know what you could have been thinking of, running off with that Indian boy in the middle of the night. You've made a shambles of your reputation, and you've made me the laughingstock of my bridge club." He glanced at her, his eyes dancing. "And your dad." He continued in a fatherly bass. "I'll shoot him myself, soon as the sheriff turns him loose. He's gonna pay for what he did to my little girl."

Giggling, Elaina accepted the plate he handed her. "This sounds great! But it's not Marie; it's Margaret. What did he do?"

"I don't know, and I don't *want* to know," the gruff voice bellowed. "All I know is, you've been smiling like the Mona Lisa ever since they brought you back here. You wipe that smile off your face and show the proper signs of complete humiliation. As for the Indian, he dies at sunup."

"I think you'd be doing him a favor if you shot him before his Uncle Joe got his hands on him."

"My Uncle Joe," Sky acknowledged with a nod, slipping into his uncle's character. "Have you been out in the sun too long, nephew? Did my sister look the full moon in the face when she was pregnant with you? A jackass would be ashamed to claim you as one of its relations."

Her hand shook with her laughter, and she sloshed the water she was trying to pour into tin mugs. It hissed on a hot rock. "We'll have to become hermits after this," she decided.

"Or we can join the circus."

"Or go to Hollywood."

"Where we'd fit right in with the rest of the crazies." He reached for the coffee she handed him, taking the cup gingerly by the hot metal handle. "Writers have to be a little crazy, too, don't they?"

"A little," she admitted. "But I've never met anyone as crazy as you are. I can't believe you stole all this stuff—three horses and all this equipment—and took off in the middle of the night."

"Me?" he exclaimed, convinced of his innocence. "Look who's sitting right across from me! I can't believe you came with me."

She sipped her coffee, and he sipped his. She looked at him, and he stared back. She grinned slowly, and he grinned back. "I can't either," she said finally. "But that's what makes it so much fun."

They packed up and remounted, and it wasn't long before they heard hoofbeats along the trail below them. The staccato sound echoed through the valley, announcing John Gray Bear's approach. Sky allowed John a glimpse of them before he packed Elaina off to higher elevations, ignoring John's "Hey, Sky! Sky!" He decided to stash the packhorse in some trees and tease John a little. Elaina watched from a sheltered vantage point while Sky doubled back and appeared on another ledge. The rock face was too steep for John to give chase. "We gotta stay together, Sky! You can't just . . . Hey, Sky, come on back!"

"I'm taking a side trip, John."

"I can't let you do that. Not with . . ."

He couldn't stop him, either. John knew that and so did Sky, but John would give it a shot, because he could use the money O'Malley was willing to pay for the return of his wife's Hollywood cousin. Shaking his head when Sky disappeared from the ledge, John plodded along the trail, looking for a way to get higher.

Leading the packhorse, with Elaina following close behind, Sky fixed his mind on a campsite he recalled as being especially beautiful. He knew he was on the right track, but it had been a long time since he'd been there. Joe had shown him the spot years ago, and it was far above the trail they used for packing. He was sure John didn't know it, and he doubted that Rick did, either. Joe had favored Sky with his secret spots long before Rick had been allowed to accompany them on their high country excursions. Sky thought of those days often, times when he and Joe had been able to head for the high country with no explanations and no itinerary, leaving Jenny with a lapful of kids. In those days, for some reason, she hadn't complained. It had been up to Joe to teach his sister's oldest son all he knew, and that responsibility was one he had never questioned.

Joe had told him more times than he could count that it was a man's world up here—all the fish and game you could want, no nagging, no bawling kids. Sky had never completely understood the comment. Joe and Jenny had always gotten along as well as any married couple he knew, but now he realized that it wasn't a need to get away from Jenny or the kids. It was the world's demands that Joe needed to leave behind periodically, and taking a horse above the highways and beyond the trails was the best way to escape.

Sky glanced back at Elaina and smiled. "How's my guest doing?" he asked, noting a droop in her posture that hadn't been there before.

"Fine."

"Tired?"

"Maybe a little."

"You shouldn't be gallivanting around at three o'clock in the morning. Wears a person out."

"No kidding." She smiled. The way he tucked his chin and flashed his eyes at her made it impossible not to. He wore a straw cowboy hat and a denim jacket over a plaid Western shirt, and he looked the part of a mountain guide. No wonder those moviemakers were so anxious to cast him in this setting. Just being teased by him was exciting, and the thought of sharing a tent with him gave her a deliciously uneasy feeling.

"Don't worry. I know where I'm going, and I think I know how to get there. It's a terrific spot by a little waterfall."

"Do you think we're being followed?"

"Not exactly. John's traveling parallel to us. He has no idea where we are, but he'll give it a few hours to make it look good before he gives up and goes home."

"I hope O'Malley pays him for his efforts."

"He will. O'Malley needs all the friends he can get."

Sky wondered whether somewhere at work in him there might be the need for a friend. Bringing a woman along hadn't been part of the scheme when he'd come up here with Joe, and it hadn't been on Sky's mind when he'd headed east out of L.A., driving like a man obsessed and begrudging every stop he had to make for gas. He hadn't wanted a friend then. He'd wanted the familiar smoky interior of Shorty's Bar, the unpretentious pine walls of Silver Moon Lodge and the unspoiled trails of the Big Horns. If he rode north, he'd cross the state line and be in Crow country, where he could probably lose himself for weeks and not see another living soul. So why had he brought this woman along?

"I guess we all do." He turned in the saddle and saw that her yellow hair caught pieces of sunshine at the crown. Her eyes brightened when he looked at her, and she clarified, "Need friends."

"Even crazy friends?"

She thought for a moment, frowning. "Just how crazy are you?"

"How crazy am I?" he echoed broadly. Slowing his mount's gait, he waited for Elaina to move into position beside him as they crossed a mountain meadow. "I'm sooo crazy that my mother says I'm just like my great-grandfather, who was a contrary."

"Quite contrary?" she teased.

"Surely a widely read Indian scholar like yourself knows what a contrary was."

She shifted in her saddle, trying to rid herself of a growing discomfort. Her legs were beginning to feel like jelly, which was certainly not the image she'd had when picturing herself riding a horse. "I suppose he was a pain in the—"

Sky laughed. "The pain in your butt isn't *my* fault, lady. You came along with me, which probably means you're just as contrary as I am."

"If I hadn't, you'd have kidnapped me."

He nodded. "Tied a rope around your hands and dragged you along behind my horse."

"Did they really do that?"

"They must have," he assured her. "I've done that scene at least three times myself."

"What about your great-grandfather?"

"He'd have put you on the horse, tied up his own hands and let you pull him." He shrugged, then stood in the stirrups to stretch his legs. "He was a contrary. They did everything backwards. It was considered a sacred role for a man to assume, sort of balancing everything out for the rest of the tribe, but it must have been hard to be so damned . . ."

"Contrary," she supplied.

"Crazy."

"Whatever. Aren't you even a little tired?" She let him see that she was by allowing a hint of supplication to creep into her voice.

"Maybe a little. I suppose we could pull over at the next rest area."

"Thank God," Elaina breathed.

They stopped to share a cold lunch. Then, while Elaina rested and watched her horse graze beside the packhorse, Sky played games with John Gray Bear. Sky was satisfied when John headed east, diligently following the trail he thought Sky had taken. It was a trail that would eventually cross the packing parties.

The spot, when he found it, was just as he had remembered it. Cool, quick mountain water cut a path between grassy banks, cascaded over a four-foot rock face, then rushed around a tree-lined bend to cut through a meadow. Sky chose a stand of tall pines for their campsite. The horses were unsaddled and hobbled before they were left to graze. Together Sky and Elaina pitched the tent, dug a small firepit and gathered wood.

"Can we go for a walk?" Elaina asked as they surveyed the job they'd done.

"We can do anything your heart desires, Miss Delacourte." His smile suggested a wide range of possibilities. "You're a paying guest, and I'm an experienced guide."

"Good," she said, more casually than she felt. "Then guide me to some game."

"Game? You want to shoot something?"

"With my camera. Do you think you could take a picture of me by the waterfall?"

"Do you think you could smile?"

She hadn't realized she wasn't. Her thoughts were elsewhere. She was standing by a tent that she would eventually get around to sharing with an *experienced* guide. For all her professional fantasizing, she wasn't very experienced, not with men. She'd have to stand her ground, she decided. The mere fact that she was alone with him didn't mean she would consent to whatever he had in mind. Yes, she could smile, she thought, and she did. She was in control.

"Very nice," he said. "Very photogenic. Hold that pose until I string the food above the bears' reach."

They trekked upstream, snapping her picture at the waterfall and meandering into thicker woods as the elevation increased. There were no paths, and the climb grew steeper, prompting Sky to help Elaina over the rough spots. He reached for her hand when her legs couldn't quite make the stretch over a rock. Then, when she teetered on top of it, the smooth soles of her boots slipping over the surface, she reached for his waist to steady herself. Reaching for each other became automatic, and when they came to a spot where woods met meadow on level ground, they were holding hands for the simple enjoyment of it.

Sky touched her shoulder, then pointed to a bull elk grazing in the meadow. The elk lifted his shaggy neck just as Elaina raised her camera, and she knew she had a perfect shot of the gracefully curved antlers against yellow-green grass. She was able to snap three pictures before he trotted out of range.

Elaina was exhausted when they reached the top, but Sky was eager to show her how far they'd come. He took her hand and pulled her along behind him. It wasn't until they stood at the edge of the rocky precipice overlooking a blue-green panorama that she understood his excitement. The height caught her by surprise, and she leaned toward him unconsciously when her legs suddenly turned to slush. Grinning, he tucked her under his arm.

"Well, what do you think? Isn't this great?"

"It's . . . a lot of . . . down," she managed.

"Afraid of heights?"

"Not . . . usually."

"If you look straight down, you'll see that this is a few hundred feet of sheer rock face."

Elaina lowered her eyes without budging her chin. Way down below her toes, there was a blur of green. "Oooh."

"Don't look down."

"You *told* me to."

"I said *if* you look straight down. I don't want to look straight down, either. It makes me feel funny." She glanced up, frowning at him, because he wasn't supposed to feel funny. She counted on him not feeling funny as she hung on to him. He laughed, tossing his head back and enjoying the cool breeze as it lifted his hair off his forehead. "Look across the valley at the mountains, the way they rise up and punch the sky," he told her. "They have such power."

"Such permanence," she added. "I like that."

He squatted suddenly, pulling Elaina with him. She gasped, steadying herself by grabbing his denim jacket. Peering into the valley, Sky chuckled. "There's ol' lonesome John, still at it."

Elaina searched in the direction of Sky's pointing finger until she spotted the tiny horseman on a distant ledge. "He's way off, isn't he?"

"Way off. There's a lake over that way, one of my favorite fishing spots. We don't take guests up there. He'll check it out today, and we'll head over there tomorrow. How's that?"

She nodded, glancing up to find his dark eyes studying her as they knelt together near the edge of the world. He'd pulled her under his arm, and he still held her. He'd spoken of power, and it was there in his face—in the strong, angular planes and the thick, dark eyebrows shielding jet black eyes from the sun. His eyes had such strength. Dark and deep, with the magnetism of mystery, they bade her to look down, deep inside him.

"Fine," she said.

"How's this?"

His mouth was hard on hers, and then softer, as the pressure eased and he leaned back, drawing her over him. It was her mouth that covered his as his tongue offered a delicate invitation. Her lips followed his as he lured them, drew them down. She knew the same slushy feeling in her stomach that she'd felt moments before in her legs. Had she leaned too far? Was she falling?

Her hair made a curtain over them, and he hooked an arm over the back of her neck to deepen their contact. She leaned over and kissed him, and he returned the pressure, slanting his mouth to taste her from a different angle. He asserted his strength, but she made him feel weak. Deliciously weak. He wasn't sure he wanted the feeling.

At her first resistance, his arm slid away, and she sat up, brushing her hair back from her face and breathing hard. "It's scary up here."

"Yeah, it is." Rolling to his feet, he offered her a hand, which she accepted unsteadily. As she stood she picked up his hat, which had fallen to the ground at some point. "Thanks," he said, settling it back on his head. "So what's next on your agenda, Miss Dela-courte?"

"My agenda?"

"We took a walk, took some pictures, shared a kiss. What's next?"

"Well, I don't think that kiss was on *my*..." He was grinning down at her, his eyes dancing with the fun of teasing her. "That was *your* idea," she reminded him as she allowed herself a smile.

"And a damn good one. An experienced guide knows how to enrich the beauty of the scenery. Course, it's been a while since I did this job full-time, so I have to kind of ease into it." He led the way down the slope, retracing their steps. "It wasn't too bad, was it? I mean considering."

"Considering what? Considering what your full-time job is now?" She laughed, unconsciously giving his hand a warm squeeze. "I'm sure you've had ample opportunity to polish up your skills before the camera."

"That's where you're wrong. I never get to kiss the girl. I may get to ravish her, but I don't get to kiss her."

"But you're an actor." She listened to the crunch of pebbles under her feet for a moment, then decided to test her preconceptions. "All actors are practiced..."

"Lovers?"

"It seems that way from what we read."

"What have you read about me?"

"Nothing."

"What have I read about you?"

Elaina frowned, first at the question, then at him. "You don't read writers' journals, do you?"

"No, but I read novels." He hiked an eyebrow and gave her a sidelong look. "Do writers research *all* their material firsthand?"

"All what material?"

"I'm on page 150."

She smiled. "When did you find the time to read?"

"Hey, for that book, honey, I'll *make* the time."

Laughing together, they swung into step hip to hip, knees flexing deeply as they tackled the steep descent.

Supper wasn't up to the standards of the previous night's Dutch-oven fare, but Sky promised fresh fish for the future. The fire was warm and comfortable, and the conversation was interspersed with long moments of the kind of quiet peculiar to the wilderness. There was a soft whisper in the trees above their heads and an occasional animal sound—a hoot or a clicking or a screech.

"What was that?"

"Probably a cat."

"House cat?"

"Mountain cat."

"Oh."

Of course it would have to be a mountain cat. What would a house cat be doing up here? Good thing she

was with an experienced guide, Elaina told herself
nervously.

"Are there any bears around here?"

"Oh, yeah. Blacks. Griz."

"They stay away from people, don't they?"

"Mostly."

"I imagine they're afraid of fire."

"Yeah."

Sky reached for the camp shovel and began sepa-
rating the coals and dousing the fire with dirt. Elaina
hugged her knees and watched.

"What'll we do . . . I mean, if, say, a bear happens
along during the night?"

"We'll be asleep."

"Well, I know, but if I hear something like a bear,
I might wake up."

"If it's a black, tell him he can have all the food he
wants if he can reach it."

"What if it's a grizzly?"

"If it's griz, tell him we're not worth his trouble.
You're too skinny, and I'd be pretty tough and stringy.
But if he'd like to come back tomorrow night, I'll fry
him up a nice batch of trout."

"You think he'll listen?"

"Hey, I'm an Indian, remember? Of course I think
he'll listen. Ready?"

"For what?"

His low chuckle sounded like one of the night
sounds, something that grew naturally out of the dark.
"For bed."

Oh, God. "In just another minute."

"Elaina."

"What?"

"There won't be any bears *inside* your tent tonight."

"You aren't sleeping outside, are you?"

The chuckle became a rolling laugh. "Not on your life. I haven't had a good night's sleep in forty-eight hours. Come on. You're tired, too. You go first, and I'll give you a minute to get changed."

He came into the tent moments later. He didn't ask whether she was ready, and he didn't warn her before he began unbuckling his belt. Why should he, she asked herself quickly, as dark as it was? Boots slid off, and the buckle clanked as jeans came down. Even with her back turned, Elaina saw each step in her mind as Sky undressed for bed. He lay down beside her, slipping into his sleeping bag. Some part of his body was near her hip. She wasn't sure what part, but she could feel the pressure and the heat of it, even through her bedroll. What would she do when he reached for her, as she ached for him to do?

"Good night, Elaina."

"What?"

"Sleep well. I'll show you more beautiful scenery tomorrow."

Chapter Five

The early morning sunlight woke Elaina. As she jacked herself up gradually on her elbows, her first thought was that the zippered tent flap did, indeed, face east. She made a mental note to see whether Sky would set the tent this way each time. He seemed to be at once amused and indignant with her when they discussed Indian customs, and she still didn't know how to characterize his attitude toward the whole issue. More observation seemed in order.

It was a good time for observation right now, in fact, as he lay sleeping beside her. She noticed that he slept on his stomach, head pillowed on folded arms. His hair curled at the back of his neck and fell in a black thatch over his forehead. His pajamas were similar to hers—white, waffle-woven thermal under-wear, which made sense for camping in the mountains, but on Sky they reminded her of a pair of cartoon character pajamas that her younger brother once had. Sky's face was as peaceful as that of a sleeping child, and only the breadth of his shoulders seemed incongruous with the image of a young boy "camping out" in the backyard with his friends.

She slipped quietly from her sleeping bag, trusting that he wouldn't choose that moment to wake up and catch her. She reached for her jeans, and he stirred. She picked up her boots, and he shifted. She eased the tent zipper down, and he groaned, but his eyelids never fluttered. There was something touching in the fact that he slept so soundly. Undoubtedly he was as tired as he'd claimed to be, and Elaina took an inexplicable satisfaction in that fact as she slid out the door. She would leave the flap open so he could greet the morning sun in whatever way was his custom.

Getting the pantry down from the trees was tricky, but Elaina had watched Sky do it, and she managed. She used gloves to prevent rope burns as she lowered the food supply to the ground. She took eggs from their specially designed plastic carton and the last of the bacon from its airtight container. Getting the fire started, setting up the cooking grate and producing a satisfactory cup of boiling water sent a feeling of self-sufficiency surging through her. She could have been one of the pioneer women she liked to write about.

Her husband might have died along the trail leaving her to make it to Oregon on her own—if she hadn't been waylaid by Sky Hunter, handsome Indian brave.

He emerged from the tent right on her mental cue. What a trooper, Elaina told herself, and she smiled. A red-and-black plaid shirt hung open over his waffle-weave long johns, and Elaina identified a toothbrush among the things he'd stuffed in his breast pocket. He yawned, stretched and ruffled his hair with his fingers.

"Good morning!" Elaina called.

"I'll let you know what I think of it after I dunk my head in the creek." He was headed in that direction.

"I've heated some water for you if you want to..." He ignored her, flopping on his belly in the dewy grass. His head disappeared. "...wash up."

Moments later he strode, dripping and smiling toward the camp fire. "Good morning! Is that bacon and eggs I smell?"

"How could you stand that co-o-ld water this early in the morning?"

"I'm a hard sleeper," he told her, peering from pan to pan to see what was cooking. "I have to take drastic measures in the morning. You said something about washing up? You didn't use the drinking water, did you?"

Pointing to a steaming bowl she'd set on a stump, she shook her head. "It's from the stream. I thought you'd want to shave or something."

She'd left a hand mirror and a comb beside the bowl, along with a plastic soapbox. He wondered if that constituted an invitation to share such personal items. Shrugging, he looked into the mirror and rubbed his chin and cheek. "Shave what?"

She handed him a steamy cup of coffee and paused to examine his face, reaching out automatically to feel its smoothness for herself. "You really don't have whiskers, do you?"

His eyes caught hers, and he gave her a lopsided grin. "I really don't."

"Except a few here . . . and here."

Her tentative fingertips tickled as they brushed over his upper lip and around his squared-off chin. "Hardly noticeable."

"You're supposed to use a couple of rocks to pluck these out," she suggested.

"You want to show me how that's done?"

"I've often wondered myself," she said slowly, tilting her head to one side as she considered. "How do you manage to trap those tiny little . . ."

"I use a disposable razor. It takes three swipes." She pulled her hand back, and he grinned, eyes dancing. "Bacon's burning."

"Oh!" Elaina scurried to save her bacon and get herself back in the self-sufficiency groove. She allowed herself only an occasional glance in the direction of the tree stump, where Sky took three swipes at face, hair and teeth and came away looking as though a makeup artist had freshened his appearance.

"You think the stream is cold," he was saying as he sat down on the requisite camp log. "Wait till you try the lake. Ten minutes'll get your teeth chattering."

"I guess I really didn't come prepared to go swimming," she admitted as she handed him a plate.

He looked shocked. "No swimming in the mountain lake? That's a mandatory scene, isn't it? I believe it starts on page 122 and runs, oh, about four pages."

"It's been done," she said, turning away quickly. She decided she would raid his saddlebag when he wasn't looking and find her book. "And I don't do the same scene twice."

"I do." It had enough of a lighthearted sound to it that he decided to add, "But I try to improvise a little so I don't *look* like I'm doing the same thing twice. Take the lake scene, for instance. If the character's a white man, he goes splashing right in after her. If he's an Indian, he lurks behind the trees and watches." He grinned, as if an overhead light had just switched on. "How about we reverse the whole thing? The Indian takes a bath in the lake and the girl comes splashing in after him!"

"Not *this* girl," she assured him as she joined him with her own breakfast.

"Well, *this* Indian's taking a bath in that lake tonight, and when I go to bed, I'm gonna feel damn good and clean." He leaned forward, looking for the box of condiments, which he spied at Elaina's side. "I'm gonna *smell* clean, too. Pass the pepper, please."

Her movements were crisp as she put the pepper in his hand. "I intend to bathe in the basin using *hot* water and come out smelling like a rose."

"Did you bring along some of that rose water the girl in the book's always dumping on herself?"

"Of course not." She glanced at him, but his grin forced her eyes away quickly. "That stuff smells cheap." The corners of her mouth refused to behave, and before she knew it, she was smiling. "I brought perfume."

"He-ey! I'm impressed." Half a slice of bacon disappeared in Sky's mouth as he considered. "Old Fast Horse would have a hell of a time staying put behind that tree if he got a whiff of fancy store-bought perfume."

"*Swift* Horse was watching over her; he wasn't spying on her. And he did bathe with her—" she reached for his plate "—eventually."

Sky's eyebrows shot up. "Guess I'd better read on."

"I guess you'd better get over here and do these dishes. You're not living up to your advertising this morning."

"Yes, ma'am." He followed her to her makeshift kitchen, where she refilled the basin with fresh water and gestured that the rest was up to him. "I usually do this in the creek, scrub 'em up with sand, but since you've got it all laid out here so nice . . ."

"I think we should use *hot* water."

"*Hot* water," he mimicked, and ascertained that it was. Three swipes per plate satisfied him. "Did I tell you that breakfast was delicious?"

"No, you didn't."

"You sure know how to rattle those pots and pans," he told her as he sloshed some soapy water around in a mug. "Ever been married?"

"No." Not exactly, she added mentally. The law said she hadn't. "Have you?"

"Yeah, once. For a couple of years."

She brought him the frying pan, and he glanced down at it, wrinkling his nose. "What happened?"

"She wanted to stay within a ten-mile radius of her birthplace and raise kids."

"And you?"

"I wanted to get as far away from the reservation as I could and raise my self-esteem." The frying pan got its three swishes. "I figured a pile of money might do it for me."

"And did it?"

"It took a while before I saw anything like a pile of money. By that time I'd learned the hard way about self-esteem." He handed her the pan, and it was her turn to wrinkle her nose. "I'm still learning."

"This isn't clean."

"It's better than it was."

She rolled her eyes, shook her head, then looked at him seriously again. "What are you learning?"

"How to hold out for what I really want and say no to the garbage. All kinds of garbage. I don't care about being a star, but I do care about acting."

"What if your agent can't get you what you want?"

He gave the prospect some thought. "I'll get it myself. That's something else I've learned—do-it-yourself Yankee ingenuity."

Elaina nodded, reflecting. "Sound advice. While you take care of something else, I think I'll take that advice and do these dishes over again myself."

"You're too meticulous to be an adventuress." He smiled as he handed her the job.

"They must all end up with dysentery, then."

The ride to the lake took them through breathtaking country. Elaina formed descriptions in her head, and most of them centered on the infinite variety of shades of green. There were carpets of young yellow-green shoots with thick patches of perennially gray-green sage. Showy alfalfa blended its purple with green, and the sweet clover ran like a yellow streak of gaiety through the tan crested wheat grass. The pine trees added stronger green statements, while stands of white birch kept their softer green hues to themselves. Even the rocks sported milky green lichen like splashes of camouflage.

Saddle weariness might have become a problem for Elaina had Sky not taken time to stop and rest, to share a dried fruit snack or a drink of water, or just to get down and lead the horses now and then. Her bot-

tom was a little tender at this point, and she appreci-
ated the chance to exercise different muscles in her legs
once in a while. Sky never asked, but he seemed to
know when she'd been sitting long enough.

He never tired of pointing out special bits of beauty,
either—the hawk gliding overhead, the scampering
ground squirrel in the pine forest, the young mule deer
in the meadow. She saw that he was as fascinated as
she was, though she had no doubt he'd seen these
sights many times before. She'd been in the Minnesota woods often enough, but she knew she'd have to
consider herself as just a city girl who'd spent a lot of
time dreaming of the wildness she'd find in the West.
She'd been west before, but she'd never been privy to
wildness, never shared it quite this way.

Of all the dreams she'd put on paper, she'd never
dreamed of anything quite as beautiful as Sky's lake.
It was a small pocket of blue water tucked behind a
ridge and surrounded by meadow and pine. Across the
lake stood a vista of granite peaks, some saw-toothed,
some square-topped, dappled with patches of snow.
Elaina was struck with the sense that it had been quiet
here forever.

She'd said little during the past hour, and Sky knew
she must have been glad they'd reached their destina-
tion, though she never complained. If she'd been a
complainer, they would have turned around a long
time ago. No, she was a wonderer. Everything she saw
was a wonder to her, and she seemed to be interested
in everything he chose to tell her. He was comfortable

with that. He watched her survey the scene, her eyes bright with enjoyment, and he decided that looking at her was equally enjoyable. Her nose and cheeks had turned pink from the sun, and her eyes were the same color as the lake. Pink and blue. Romantic colors. Romantic. That was the only part that bothered him. She was too damned romantic.

He knew he was playing to just that part of her nature, and he wasn't sure he liked himself for it. He reminded himself that she was, first and foremost, a beautiful woman, and she enjoyed his company. He did all the right things to ensure that she would find him intriguing. It was a role he played well, and he slipped into it easily with her because the right chemistry had been there from the beginning. They would give each other more enjoyment yet, Sky decided as he swung down from his saddle, maybe even some pleasant memories.

"How good a fisherman are you, Elaina?" he asked, breaking into her reverie as she looked out over the lake. "Can you cast?"

"I might be able to sit on the bank and direct." Her heel dragged across her mount's rump, but the horse stood quietly. She'd thought she was doing pretty well in the saddle, and she glanced over her shoulder to see whether Sky had noticed that sometime in the past hour or two her muscles had turned to mush.

He was busy untying his saddlebags, however. "You, too? Seems like everybody wants to direct these days."

"I wouldn't want to catch something and have to take it off the hook."

"Or clean it?"

"Or even cook it," she admitted.

"I don't suppose you'd mind eating it, though."

"Not if you did the rest." She ducked under his palomino's neck and came up smiling. "I'm a paying guest. Remember?"

He noticed how closely her hair matched his horse's sun-gold coat. "I cook better than I clean up."

"I don't mind assisting."

"Ah, a hook baiter. Just what I need." If she wanted to play it coy, that was fine with him, but he was willing to call a spade a spade. He stripped the gear from his horse's back, and Elaina turned to her own mount to follow suit.

"Tell you what," she ventured as she struggled under the weight of bags and saddle. "You take care of the fish from start to finish, and I'll set up camp. I think I know exactly what goes where now."

"The woman finally learns her place," he told his palomino. "Tent door facing east, remember."

"I remember." She placed her load carefully on the ground. "I also remember you completely missing sunrise this morning."

After dumping his gear next to hers, he straightened and took a step closer, so that she had to look up at his easy smile. "Not *completely*. Your pajamas are pretty much like mine, only they fit you tighter." She scowled up at him, and he laughed.

"You'd better hope you can con some fish into taking your bait."

"You'd better hope I can, too."

Smiling to herself as she set about her chores, she enjoyed the modern version of a scene she'd often described. In times long past the woman set up the tent and tended the fire, while the man went out to catch supper. The arrangement was exciting—two people pooling the best of their efforts in the interest of survival. Such was the stuff her romances were made of. The idea had elemental appeal, and here in the mountains the beauty and simplicity of it became real. She would have enjoyed being one of her own heroines.

She took her camera with her down to the lake and found Sky standing in crystal-blue lake water up to his buttocks. Gently rippling water gleamed silver around the rubberized waders that made it easier for him to bear the cold for long, leisurely hours of fishing. He seemed completely content, absolutely at peace as he cast his line and patiently reeled it in. The click and whir that accompanied each shot she took didn't distract him. He fished until he brought in several pan-sized trout, and then he waded ashore in triumph.

He swung a stringer of three silvery fish under her nose and crowed, "Fresh out of the tank. Stoke up the fire and put on the coffee, honey. I'm bringing home a feast."

"Whew!" Her nose wrinkled prettily. "I'm glad you're taking care of the technical part."

"Like chopping off the heads and spilling out the guts?" She turned the corners of her mouth down and nodded. "You won't even have to look. I'll take them away from the camp and do the honors. Keeps the woman happy and keeps the varmints away."

"I did get everything unpacked and started the fire." Falling into step beside him as he slogged along the bank in his waders, she wondered, "What varmints?"

"The ones who like fish. Coons, cougars, bears..."

"Think they'll smell the cooking?"

"Might."

"Think they'll come around?"

"Might."

Elaina surveyed the ground and spied a stout stick, which she snatched up immediately. "I'll be ready for them."

Grinning, Sky winked his approval, and she walked to her outdoor hearth with a light heart. A few moments later Sky appeared with fillets of trout, which he promptly popped in a pan.

Perched on a log, Elaina set her chin in her hands and watched him prepare supper.

As he turned the fish with his right hand, he gave a sudden snap of his fingers with the left. "Oh, geez, I should've remembered—being from Minnesota, I'll bet you're some kind of Scandinavian, huh?"

"My mother's Norwegian. Why?"

"I should have left the heads on the fish. Don't you guys eat the eyes?" Elaina gave him a funny pop-eyed frown. "I'm sure Scandinavians are supposed to like fried fish eyes."

"Where'd you hear that?"

"I came across it in my reading," he said seriously. "Some *research* I did once."

"For... school or something?" She scooted to the outer curve of the log and leaned forward, enjoying the smell of fish frying outdoors.

"For my own edification," he told her, flipping another fillet. "Thought I might write a book about some kind of Scandinavians—Norwegians, Swedes, whatever. I figure they're probably pretty close. Fried fish eyes." His eyes danced when he glanced up from his task. "You probably like them with hardtack and meatballs, right?"

"That's probably Swedish," she decided, her back stiffening slightly. One Scandinavian, after all, was *not* the same as another. "I don't know anything about any fried fish eyes. Or any Swedes, for that matter. I'm Norwegian and Irish."

"Delacourte?" Sky registered the information with a raised brow. "Interesting. Well, I'm certain you're supposed to like fried fish eyes. I did come close to trying some *lutefiske* once. That's Norwegian fish, isn't it?" Elaina nodded. "Couldn't get past the smell."

She laughed. "You have such a well-developed sense of smell. How can you stand the smell of tripe?"

"You mean *taniga*?" She nodded. "Stomach and intestine of cow."

"Buffalo," she corrected.

"Wake up, girl," he said, shaking his head as he slid the fillets onto plates. "Nobody gets any buffalo in his cooking pot these days. Ever tried any *taniga*?" She shook her head, wondering if he'd offer that for tomorrow night. She wasn't sure.... "Then what do *you* know?"

"I've read about it," she insisted.

"And I've read about fish eyes. Come on, confess. I know you like them."

"All right, all right." She gave in, laughing. "I agree. *Lutefiske* stinks."

"So does *taniga*. How do you like rainbow trout?" He lowered the plate, waving it back and forth under her nose.

"It smells...mmmmm..."

"Mouth-watering?" She nodded. "Marvelous?" Elaina nodded again and took the plate. "A hell of a lot better than *lutefiske* or *taniga*," he concluded, reaching for his own plate. "But next time I'll save you the eyes. We like to keep the paying guests happy."

He served the fish with fruit compote and sourdough bread. Elaina made coffee, and they lingered over two cups apiece, teasing each other and laughing, confessing to preconceptions and then laughing some more. Elaina boiled lake water and scoured the dishes to her satisfaction, while Sky weighed the pros of having a cigarette against the cons and found the cons to be heavier. The air was too good to tamper with here. Maybe he would finally kick the habit. He disdained habits, anyway, and he didn't know why he held on to that one.

"I'm heading for the lake for a quick bath before the sun goes down," Sky announced. "You can cover your face or join me, however the spirit moves you."

Elaina glanced at the tranquil blue water. "You'll freeze."

"Actually, the water feels warmer in the evening. It holds on to the day's sunshine while the air in the daytime just lets the warmth slip away."

He had a way of turning a phrase that made his ideas almost irresistible, but Elaina told herself to stand her ground. "I'll heat my water over the coals, thank you."

"Suit yourself," he said, rising to his feet. "I won't mind if you peek—as long as it's strictly in the interests of research."

"I have a Gray's *Anatomy* at home."

His grin was wicked. "Yeah, but you don't have a Gray Bear's *Anatomy*. For all you know, I might have some extra parts."

Her grin matched his. "Or you might be short some."

Sky laughed as he left the camp, and Elaina heard his laughter twice more as she set about heating her bathwater. She arranged her soap and toiletries on the stump she was using for a washstand and began washing, admitting to herself that the method was indeed unsatisfactory. A real bath would feel good, even a cold one, and the lake water was remarkably clean and clear. Maybe later, after Sky went to bed. She took up the basin and moved to empty it, not totally unaware that she was walking toward the lake. Sheltered by pines, she bent to pour the water out, straightened slowly, and cast a furtive glance at the lake.

Sky was swimming toward shore. Powerful strokes propelled him through the water until he was ten feet from the bank. He stood suddenly, water sluicing down his body, and he swept the hair back from his face. The waterline hit him just below the navel. He was smooth skinned, bronze, sleek and slim hipped, the water glinting in the low sunlight as it beaded on his shoulders. He slid his hands down his face and looked up at the shoreline, his eyes zooming in on hers like a powerful camera lens. She couldn't breathe, couldn't move, as they exchanged a frank stare. And then *he* moved, one step, two, and she watched, mesmerized. Finally she turned, an abrupt movement, and stumbled toward the camp fire.

He was dressed when he appeared before her again, his hair a mop of wet tendrils, not a hint of a smile on his face. She waited for the bomb to drop, for him to tease her, mock her. He didn't. They sat for a time in silence while the fire died and the last of the daylight slipped away. Then she busied herself with the cookware and utensils, and he restored the supplies in the panniers and took them from the tent. When he returned he found Elaina curled up in her bedroll. He smiled to himself as he stripped off his clothes and rolled into his bed.

She thought he was asleep. He'd been still for some time, and his breathing was quiet and steady. Everything, in fact, seemed still—the air, the trees outside. She strained to listen to the gentle lapping of the lake's water. It would be chilly, but Sky had said it wouldn't feel as cold as it might during the day, when the sun favored air over water. She could almost feel the water slipping over her, cooling her skin, which felt tight and sticky as she lay there in the little tent. It was the still air and the small, confining tent that made her restless, she decided. Quickly and quietly she gathered her jeans, shirt and boots, and crept away from the tent.

The water near the edge of the lake reached to the middle of her thighs. Elaina stepped gingerly, feeling for rocks with her feet. There was fine gravel in most places, but her toes met an occasional rock, and she decided to paddle above all that, though she planned to even stick close to the bank. The moon made a silver trail across the water, which led Elaina's eyes to the opposite shore, where a family of deer seemed to drink moonlight from the lake. Elaina drifted in the water, challenging herself to make no sounds that might scare them away. She realized she felt comfortable below the waterline as her body temperature adjusted to that of the lake. Occasionally she felt something slide past her leg, and she decided not to think about what it was. The sensation itself was only a tickle.

When the deer retreated from the water's edge, Elaina retrieved her shampoo from a grassy spot on shore and washed her hair. Then she let herself drift near the bank, where a large rock just below the water's surface gave her a mooring. With her eyes closed she listened to the soft night sounds—crickets, a little flutter or rustle now and then, and the slight whisper of stirring pines. When she heard the quiet ripple of a body entering the water, she kept her eyes closed. At that moment she admitted to herself that she'd known he would come.

His body slid over hers as she imagined a seal or an otter might greet its mate in the water. Her rock helped her stay afloat, and he found it, too, braced himself on it, and kissed her. It was during their kiss that their feet touched the bottom of the lake, their arms encircled each other, and wet skin made prickly magic over wet skin. At last they gasped for air, as though they both had gone under.

"You're supposed to stand behind the tree and look out for me," she managed, sliding her hand over the satin of his shoulder. Her breasts met his chest, trapping a little reservoir between them.

"Is that what you were doing for me earlier?"

"I think so."

"I don't think so. I think only Fast Horse manages an act like that."

"*Swift* Horse," she whispered.

"Swift Horse ain't too swift. Cold, black ink courses through his veins." He smoothed his hand over her cap of wet hair. "Silky. It smells like coconut. I watched you wash it." With a wistful smile he brushed a drop of water from the point of her chin with his thumb. "I did watch over you for a while—until I couldn't stand it anymore. I've never seen anyone look so beautiful." He put his lips against her neck and whispered again, "Beautiful," and she shivered.

"And you aren't missing any parts," she commented with a smile.

"Anatomy is anatomy." He gave a deep, satisfied laugh as he felt her hands explore his back. "I haven't got anything extra, either."

"You were right about the bath," she said, her throat inexplicably dry. "It feels good to be . . ."

His body barely brushed against hers below the water. "Oh, yeah, it does."

"You weren't asleep."

"Uh-uh." Of course not. After he'd seen the look on her face when he'd emerged from his bath, had she expected him to crawl into the sack and go to sleep? He slid one hand to the small of her back, pulled her close and told her that this, *this*, was how much sleep he could get lying next to her.

"Why didn't you tell me before?" she whispered, her breath teasing his chin.

"You didn't ask. If you had, I'd have told you. I want to make love to you."

"Oh, Sky, I don't . . ."

"Yes, you do." His mouth came down hard on hers, and he felt the hunger already clamoring inside him. He experienced the feel of her by stages, from his thighs to his belly to his chest, all pressed against her. She was warmer than the water that surrounded him, softer than its caress, shier than its gentle lapping. She was woman; she was what he had been missing for longer than he knew. He needed her.

"I'm . . . not prepared."

"I am."

"Sky, please . . ."

"I will. I promise."

Chapter Six

L et me bathe you."

She was stiff. He would make her supple. The shampoo lay where he'd seen her leave it, and he reached for the bottle, then poured the liquid out until it filled his cupped palm. He loved the smell of coconut.

She shivered with cold. He would make her tremble with heat. He stood facing her in the water at the edge of the lake, in the trail of moonlight, and he dribbled thick liquid coconut over her shoulders, breasts and back. She looked up at him, her eyes filled with wonder. He pulled her into his arms and used firm, massaging strokes to work the lather over her back. She closed her eyes and dropped her head to his shoulder as he kneaded the small of her back and splayed his fingers over her buttocks. She stopped shivering.

A series of small, openmouthed kisses tantalized his chest, and he squeezed the flesh that filled his hands. Her kisses became nibbles. His chest tightened, and his flat nipples puckered. Her gesture was at once innocent and effective, and it was his turn to wonder at his own response. He turned her around, pulled her soapy back against him and resumed his ministrations from her fingertips to her shoulders, knowing that she would luxuriate in the waiting.

He would touch her breasts soon, he thought. The warm, slick pressure of his hands would glide over her aching breasts and give them the attention they craved.

Elaina let her head drop back and rest on his shoulder, fighting to contain the moan she felt rising inside her like water that would sigh in a curling wave only after it crested. Water relaxed her. Water soothed her with gentle motion, sliding motion, gliding motion, circling around her breasts and over her belly, sluicing through her.

"I love coconut," a deep voice whispered near her ear. Sky, she thought. Sky had become one with the water. "You smell like a tropical summer night." He pressed a kiss just below her earlobe and took her breasts in his hands. "Hot, sultry night," he whispered, his voice raspy. She felt the heat he described. "The smell of ripe fruit and coconut." She gasped as his fingertips found her nipples. "I want to taste what I smell."

He slid his hands over her belly again, but this time he stretched his own imagination and hers to touch a cresting wave, to make it curl, make it break over the tips of beckoning fingers. Her mind soared on the moan she had no thought to contain.

He knew exactly where his clothes were piled with hers, and he had, indeed, come prepared, if he could find the right pocket. He was always prepared, he told himself—with the right words, the right moves, the right touch and the right protection. But as he laid her down on the grassy lakeshore, he felt a need for other words, and he wasn't sure what they were. She was the color of moonlight, a soft and fragile thing, and he knelt beside her, leaned over her and then froze. He needed a new move, one directed by a source of energy he didn't think he possessed. It unnerved him when she raised her arms, stretched them out to him and bade him come to her with whatever he had. He saw his own hands respond, but he needed something else to touch her with, and he had nothing; he'd used it all.

Protection, he thought as he fumbled around and found what he was looking for. But there was something within *him* that wanted protection from...what? From her? What could this delicate creature he'd taken from the water do to him? He wanted to provide greater protection *for* her, some kind of an umbrella that would make this a truly isolated moment, like a dream, something that affected neither past nor future. He told himself to say the magic words, the lines that would make it so.

His lines flew from his head. He had no script, no director, no cues. There wasn't even a costume—nothing to make him look like someone else, nothing to hide behind. No facade. No magic words. Confused, he glanced quickly at the grass above her head.

"Sky Hunter," she whispered, and the sound of his name reminded him of who he was. She knew it, too, he told himself, and as long as she knew, it was all right. He lowered his body over hers, remembered that he was an actor, a fact that, he tried to convince himself, she accepted with the utterance of his name.

She received him without conditions or restraint. Guilelessly open, she met his pace easily, because it was what she needed it to be. Slow, deep, all-consuming, the motion of his body polarized thought and sensation, deadening the one and quickening the other. Artless, trusting, wide with wonder, her eyes struck him speechless, while her body drained away all his needs and filled him with warm satisfaction.

"I feel like I didn't give you much choice," he said quietly, touching her damp hair as he held her close to his side.

"I wanted you," she told him.

"I made you want me."

"No. I wanted you."

He looked up at the stars and found them winking at him. Was that some kind of joke on him? "*I* wanted *you*, sure as hell."

"I guess I knew that when I agreed to come with you. I had a choice then, too."

"Okay, so that's established. How do you feel about getting in the water again?"

She shivered and tightened her arms around him. "What I'd like to do is crawl into a warm sleeping bag."

"What I'd like to do is zip the two of them together and *then* crawl in. But first I have to rinse you off." He was rolling to his bare feet and pulling her up with him. "You smell delicious, but you taste like soap."

"So?"

"So I don't think the wanting is over for tonight." He turned, saw how wistful she looked, and smiled. "Do you?"

She laughed and shook her head as she followed him into the water. The shock of its first touch made her squeal, and he laughed, too, as he swept her into his arms and carried her in.

Moments later he dried her quickly with his shirt while she dabbed at him with hers. The crack of a branch somewhere close by startled Elaina. "Could that be a bear?" she whispered.

"Yup."

"Oh, God. And we were sprawled out on the ground like a picnic lunch."

"Bears have certain standards, too, you know." He propped himself on an elbow, rearranging a pair of jeans beneath himself and smiled down at her. The lighting could have been better, he thought. The moon had just slipped behind a cloud. "They never attack a man when he's in the process of rutting."

"Rutting!"

"The meat tastes too gamy."

"So they shove the man aside and have the woman for supper, since women don't *rut*."

"No, no, they never interrupt. It's too dangerous. There's nothing more unpredictable than a male human during mating season." He touched her shoulder and ran a single finger down her arm, which she drew across her breasts with a shiver. "Scared?" he asked.

"A little."

"As long as we're making love, they won't bother us." He found her temple by nosing through wisps of hair, and he planted a kiss there. "Some things are sacred, even to bears."

"And to rutting male humans?"

Realizing that "sacred" had been a strange word for him to choose, he let her question pass. "Your skin is icy," he whispered. "Let's go back to the tent."

They pulled jeans, shirts and boots on quickly, then scurried to the tent, anxious to shed their damp clothing and slide into bed next to each other. Sky combined the two sleeping bags and turned to find Elaina holding her waffle-weave undershirt aloft.

"You're not thinking of putting that on, are you?"

Lowering her arms, Elaina tried to look past the outline of his face, but she could discern no more than that in the dark. "It *is* nice and warm."

"So am I." He flipped the covers back and drew her with him as he crawled into the bag. "I'm nice." The length of her body slid against his, and he caught his breath for a moment. "And I'm warm. I'll keep you warm."

His body did feel warm, and Elaina wondered what kind of furnace he had going inside him. Her skin was as cold as the crisp night air. "I'm not sure I can return the favor."

"You don't have to," he whispered, caressing her back as he cuddled her. "The pleasure is all mine."

The exquisite ache that sprang within her breast as he touched her said otherwise.

"It's your job to keep the bears posted on what we're doing," he told her.

His breath made a warm spot in the valley between her breasts, and she wanted him to whisper over her more. "How do I do that?"

"You make those wonderful little sounds, like you did before, when I . . ."

Taking her nipple between his lips, he taunted and teased until she heard a soft, feminine moan and was only vaguely conscious of the voice being hers.

"That's right, honey," he whispered. "Tell the bears how good it is when I touch you . . . here." He heard the catch in her breathing. "And tell *me*." She groaned. "Yes, tell me just that way."

She began to drift again, as she had in the water, each gentle caress tightening her skin as a surging feeling gradually built within her. For each of her responses he offered an even more intense temptation.

He found himself attuned to her in a way unlike he'd ever been with anyone else. The softness that quivered beneath his hands and lips became more than flesh. There was no one else for him. There was only Elaina. Elaina—innocent and trusting and willing to give, willing to take risks to... to be with him? To be with Sky? Was that her only motive? The thought sent a shaft of sensation through his chest and into his belly. It was a shaft of needs, not singular but multiple, which was sharpened by the feel of her beneath his hands, and brightened and made intensely warm by the fact that this was Elaina. He needed to be part of her, and he said her name over and over, filling her ears with the warm sound as he filled her body with his.

Sky was magic. He rose over her like a gathering storm, full of power and energy. Elaina met his energy with her own, and they clung to each other, letting the sucking, slamming surf they'd created take them up and over, then pull back in slow retreat, leaving them spent and shuddering.

Elaina slept, her cheek against Sky's chest, but her breath, puffs of warmth across his diaphragm, kept him awake, awed by what they'd shared. Ordinarily he would have sex, followed by a cigarette, and then he'd find an empty bed and go to sleep. If he were in a strange place, he'd leave. In his own home, he would seek out the guest room. He would always be tired of the perfume, whatever the brand, tired of the practiced coyness or the celluloid steaminess. He would feel crowded, drained and empty, and he'd move off to be by himself, thinking that he was damn glad that was done.

Elaina stirred and made a soft, contented sound, and Sky shifted slightly, the better to hold her close. The faint smell of coconut mingled with the musky smell of lovemaking, and he savored it. Cold lake water and silky shampoo, warm musk and satin skin next to his, and lovemaking, not simply sex. God, he felt good. Elaina was no actress, and she made him feel real.

For the first time in heaven knew how long, he hadn't worried about his performance. Nor had he been out to gratify himself, to do it because it was necessary and be done with it. He'd met her needs with his, taken her gifts and given something back in return. Gifts, real *gifts*, and he had taken his pleasure in the giving, gloried in the receiving.

He brushed her hair back from her temple and admired what he could see of her profile—the slope of her forehead, the small shadow of her nose, the curve of her cheekbone. Asleep, she was childlike in her innocence. Awake, she was bright, clever, enthusiastic and passionate, all woman, but still innocent. She believed her own romantic nonsense. She believed in hearts and flowers, bells and happily ever after. Sky wasn't happily-ever-after material, and he knew it. Her gifts were precious, and he had no damn business taking them from her. He pressed his lips against her forehead and sucked in strength with the night air as she cuddled closer to him.

It was early when Elaina woke. She was able to extricate herself from Sky without disturbing him much. He turned on his side, nuzzled his face in the flannel-lined bedding and slept on. Elaina stretched against the stiffness that had settled in her body overnight and wondered how Sky managed to look so comfortable sleeping virtually on the ground.

The air was summer-morning cordial, and Elaina was completely nude. Sitting on her heels, she glanced at her clothes and then down at herself. She knew how scandalous it was for her to wish that Sky would wake up just then and see her, too, but she did. She envisioned the smile on his face and the look in his eyes, a look she hadn't been able to see in the dark. Still, she'd felt it, and it had made her feel beautiful. Indeed, she *was* beautiful, and she wouldn't have minded if he'd opened his eyes to admire her just then.

But he didn't, and she decided to dress, find the fishing gear and surprise him with fish for breakfast. The trouble was, she didn't know the first thing about fishing, and it wasn't long before she had tangled the line without even dropping it into the water.

"Nice try." Startled, Elaina looked up from her studied effort to untangle the line. Sky strode toward her, the bottoms of his jeans swishing in the grass. It embarrassed her to have him catch her with his tangled fishing line in her lap, but he was smiling as he sank to his knees on the ground next to her. "Why didn't you wait for me to help you out with this?"

"I'm sorry. It looks so easy, and I thought I could surprise you by having a fish in the pan when you got up."

"You mean gutted and scaled?"

"I figured I could probably wear gloves and hold it at arm's length." She demonstrated.

He took the fishing line from her lap and began working at the knot as he mugged at her and drawled, "Well, this is a fine mess you've gotten us into, Stanley."

"I think I could..." He took a jackknife from his pocket and cut the line. Elaina shrugged. "I'd gotten most of it out."

He folded the long blade into the knife and put it away. "This way we'll have fish for breakfast instead of lunch." With a guarded look he added, "How are you feeling this morning?"

"Wonderful." Her smile reminded him that she had no facility with coyness. "How are you feeling?"

"Hungry, which is par for the course for me."

She felt her shoulders stiffen as she tried to concentrate on watching him reattach the hook, his fingers adroit. "Course?"

"You know, the morning after."

"Oh . . . yes." Of course, she told herself. He had those Hollywood experiences in mind. He'd made it clear that Hollywood hadn't provided the best of his memories, though. These mountains had. And there had been no mistaking his feelings last night. Her feelings had been his, just as her body had been his. He had to be feeling wonderful *and* hungry. "What would go with fish for breakfast, then? Eggs? Biscuits? I could go get them started while you—"

"Grease bread," he said flatly.

"*Grease* bread?" Her nose curled up at the very combination of words.

"You mean ol' Fast Horse never made you any *kabubu* bread?" Hook and lure firmly in place, Sky turned an inquiring eyebrow up at Elaina. "What does he feed his captives, anyway? *Wasicu* cannot live by *papa* alone."

Elaina frowned, puzzling. "I have a list of the most-used Lakota words and phrases taped right on my computer. Let's see . . . *wasicu* is white man, and . . ." He was already laughing when she snapped her fingers and pointed at him. "*Papa* is buffalo jerky!"

"Are you sure it's not 'white jerky' and 'buffalo man'? You'd better run that through the computer one more time."

"So what's grease bread like?" Her mouth had stiffened into a straight line as she stood, one hand on her hip.

"Filling." Sitting on the ground, Sky pulled his boots and socks off, then began rolling his jeans up. "I think it's a universal recipe. Hard times bread that tastes a helluva lot better when you're not eating it because you have to." He shed his shirt, gathered his fishing rod and waded into the water.

"Do we have to?"

"No, but we want to," he told her, finding his spot. "We're doing research."

"I've heard of *fry* bread," she ventured.

"Not the same." With his back to her, he prepared to cast. She thought a straw hat and a corncob pipe would fit the picture. "I imagine *kabubu* bread is sort of like the stuff Moses and his buddies ate just before he..." a flick of his wrist sent the weighted hook sailing with a whir of the reel "...parted the waters."

"Oh. I guess those were hard times."

"I guess they were. Anyway, we eat it, and we remember." He turned the crank on the reel slowly, with practiced patience.

"And appreciate what we have?"

One brawny shoulder lifted in a shrug. "Maybe, if we've come that far."

"I like that idea," she decided. "I think I'm going to like this *kabubu* bread, too."

"Not if I don't catch anything to go with it, and if I stand here talking to you, I won't. Maybe you want to go for a little hike or something, hmm? Give me half an hour or so."

Her quiet "okay" gave him a pang of guilt. He'd dismissed her, and she knew it. He listened to her retreat through the grass, stubbornly resisting the urge to call her back and offer to teach her to cast or get her to roll around with him in the dewy grass and to hell with breakfast, which was what he really wanted. Food had been the last thing on his mind when he woke up, and his thoughts hadn't changed since.

Had he actually told her to take a hike? Elaina wondered as she strode along the bank. Did he really want to spend this morning fishing? How was he able to send her away when she wanted nothing more than to bask in his presence this morning? She came to the place where they'd bathed the night before. Here was where she'd stood while he dried her off, and there was the nest they'd made in the grass. A short distance away she noticed a huge flat rock that sat in the water like a table, only a few yards from shore. If she couldn't bask in his presence, she decided, she'd bask in the sun.

Her fantasy dictated that she should strip down completely and parade around in the wilderness, unashamed. The sun was bright, getting warmer, the sky clear and blue—perfect. Only the wildlife would be there to witness her boldness. Many times she'd imagined herself doing just that in broad daylight. She glanced toward a stand of pines and then at the rock, and decided she'd just roll her pants up and wade out.

The water was a little deeper than she'd expected, and she ended up wet to the middle of her butt, but she managed to hoist herself up to the rock's surface without much difficulty. It was lovely. It was peaceful. Not a soul around. Of course, Sky *might* find his way to the same spot, as he had the night before, but...probably not. He was busy fishing. He loved to fish. Elaina took a deep breath and unbuttoned her blouse.

She was lying in the sun when he came looking for her, and she was gloriously nude. Her sun-drenched hair spilled across her bed of granite; her eyes were closed, and every inch of her skin drank in the morning. Sky stared at her, filling his brain with the image of her from his vantage point on a sparsely wooded knoll. He was stupefied. She could have been an advertisement for something. What? Suntan lotion? Sunglasses? She appeared to have neither, and she was probably burning every physical asset God had given her. More likely a scent—he suddenly smelled coconut—or lip gloss. She had perfectly shaped lips. Maybe an ad for diet soda. Or simply one for womanhood.

A smile touched the corners of his mouth. Simply. That was a laugh. It used to be *simply*. He remembered how the stars had laughed at him the night before, and he knew that had been some sort of inside joke. Everything he thought a woman should be was lying down there on top of her jeans instead of inside them, and he was standing up here with sweaty palms and a dry throat. He felt like a kid.

So what was he going to do about this lucky find? Damn him, he'd done enough already. He figured it wouldn't hurt to admire her just a minute longer. After all, even ol' Fast Horse wasn't above taking inventory from behind a tree. Then he'd go back to the campsite and wait for her, and when she came back, he'd fry her up some breakfast. And then he'd take her back to the packing party so she could finish out the rest of her vacation without his brand of complication.

Dressed and headed in the direction of the campsite, Elaina wondered if she might have overdone the sunning just a bit. She hadn't intended to stay out there very long, but the sun had felt so good. A little voice in the back of her head chided her. Had she thought Sky might come looking for her? Of course not! He was fishing, and she'd known she had some time to herself, that no one would see her. Still, that fantasy of him wading out to the rock, reaching, touching... She shook her head, banished the fantasy and strode purposefully to the campsite.

"I see you had good luck."

"What?" Sky looked up from his cooking, half hoping to see her exactly as he'd seen her on the rock. She was wearing her jeans, of course, but they were wet and clinging, as was her blouse. She looked no less desirable. He forced his eyes to return to the frying fish. "Oh, yeah, it didn't take long. Been swimming?"

"I was sort of...wading. I got my clothes a little wet."

"Maybe you'd better change them. I'm almost done here."

Sitting next to him on the log in front of the fire, she shrugged and peered into the pan that held something that looked like a fried Frisbee. "They'll dry. Is this it? The *kabubu* bread?"

"That's the stuff. Think you can handle it?"

"It looks harmless enough."

He chuckled as he slid golden-brown fish from pan to plate. "If we can't eat it, we can try skipping it on the lake. Joe set the record at six skips with an eight-incher."

"Really?" She looked back at the bread and imagined its course.

"Yeah, really. That's another whopper for you."

She accepted the plate, studying the fish and the flat, heavy-looking bread. "It sounded plausible enough. Where are my eyes?"

"In your pretty little head," he said absently as he got ready to test his own cooking.

"I mean my fish eyes. You promised."

"Oh, right." He reached for a covered pan.

"I'm kidding," she said quickly, wincing as he whipped off the cover and shoved it under her nose.

"So am I." She looked up and caught a wink from him. "Stewed apples."

"You're a terrible tease."

"I know." He spooned apples onto her plate. "How much? Little bit? Whole bunch?"

She'd heard that expression at Silver Moon, and she filed it now in her mental drawer full of colloquialisms. "That's plenty. What are we doing today? Heading north?"

"Heading southeast. We should meet up with Rick's group by tonight, if they didn't waste too much time looking for us."

There was nothing lighthearted in his tone. She glanced at him, frowning slightly. "You're teasing again, aren't you?"

"No." He concentrated on his plate, taking another forkful of fish.

"But I don't want to go back. I mean I...I'd rather not travel with a group anymore."

"It's safer with a larger group. You keep talking about bears, and I keep making light of it, but the truth is..." He looked up, saw the hurt in her face and hated himself for putting it there. "The truth is, you're better off with the group."

"I'm not afraid anymore," she said quietly.

"Maybe you should be."

There was no mistaking his meaning. His "morning after" feeling was, indeed, as unpleasant as a hangover, and he'd long since chosen abstinence over hangovers. Elaina sensed all this and wasn't pleased. She packed her gear without a word. She would not be resentful, she told herself. She'd done what she'd done because she'd felt good about him, and she had no apologies to make for feeling that way. It was Sky Hunter who was behaving like the fool, she told herself. She knew he'd felt something for her, too.

Sky chose a shortcut down the mountain, and he led the way, letting Elaina lead the packhorse. It was a little steep, a little narrow, maybe a little rockier than he would have liked, but he figured it might put them in touch with Rick's party before dark. If not, he'd take Elaina back to Silver Moon and refund her money himself. Of course, if he knew anything about the woman, and at this point he thought he did, her money wasn't uppermost on her mind. What he'd taken from her couldn't be refunded. The question of what she might have taken from him tickled the edge of his thoughts, but he refused to consider it.

The light aircraft registered only as a distant buzzing sound until it was too late. By the time Sky realized that the plane was diving at their backs just for a lark, the horses had already decided they were being attacked. They were immune to most mountain hazards, but not to this one. Sky was out of his saddle in an instant, and his palomino was gone in the next.

"Get down!" He saw the sudden terror in the black's eyes, his eyeballs rimmed in white. Elaina's eyes looked the same way. Sky's gut knotted. "The high side!" he shouted as he twisted the blade on his jackknife and dived for the packhorse's lead rope.

The black laid back his ears just as Elaina swung down, lost her grip and slid to the ground. Out of the corner of his eye Sky saw her go down beneath the flailing hooves. Stop the packhorse, he thought. He'll trample her. As the plane buzzed a tree and soared off, Elaina's mount took off after the palomino. The packhorse skittered, hindered by Sky's hold. Elaina lifted her face from the dirt and saw the underside of the horse's belly and Sky's legs on the far side—the low side of the trail. A rope dangled near her hand.

"Whoa, boy," she managed as she reached for it, rising to one knee.

"Out of the way, Elaina."

"Sky!"

The horse's hindquarters swung wide, and there was nothing beneath Sky's boot heels except empty air. He stumbled, tried to catch himself, and then disappeared over the edge.

Chapter Seven

Sky!"

The packhorse backed up a few steps, then stopped as Elaina stumbled past him. The edge of the trail loomed close, three steps away, maybe four, and beyond that edge a distant mountain top, the blur of evergreen. Her knees refused to hold her.

"Skyyyyy!"

It was a thin screech, creating a desperate echo. She scrambled over the gravel, unable to make her feet move efficiently, unable to utter another intelligible sound. Hovering at the edge of the chasm on her hands and knees, she whimpered and rocked forward.

His body lay thirty feet below her on a slanted outcrop. Elaina's heart raced in her chest like a freight train, and a whoosh of terror roared through her head, making her dizzy. But the trail didn't drop off at a ninety degree angle as she'd imagined. Though the incline was steep, it looked as though he might have rolled, or slid, at least part of the way.

"Sky?" Hope edged out the terror in her voice. "Sky, answer me, please. Pleeease." Eyes shut tight, Elaina forced a prayer through gritted teeth. "Please, God…" Then she thought she heard a groan. "Sky?" The next groan was a genuine attempt to respond. "Thank God," she breathed, and the words echoed in her ears. "You're alive."

"If you say so," he managed, lifting his head and pulling one knee underneath him.

"Be careful!" she gasped, reaching automatically with one ineffectual hand. "Oh, Sky, please don't move. There's another…you're too close to the edge. You can't move!"

"I don't think I want to stay here," he informed her calmly without looking up.

"No!" Calm down, she told herself, and she tried the word again. "No, I don't blame you. I'm going to…" *What am I going to do?* "I'm going to pull you up."

He lifted his face, and she saw blood, along with a sardonic smile. "Was that wishful thinking or comic relief?"

"It's a plan—the only one I've got. Now you just..." Rocking back on her heels, Elaina looked around in a desperate search for help. And there it stood, beautifully docile, gloriously unaffected by commotion. "The packhorse!"

"Talk to him," she heard Sky say as she rose slowly from the ground. "Nice and easy. Don't scare him."

"Whoa, boy. Let me get that stuff off you." He'd been a dull, unremarkable beast of burden before this moment, but now the gray packhorse was a miracle. He stood, ground-tied by the lead rope, his neck drooping near his knees, and he made no move to dodge Elaina's claim on him. "Good boy. You have to help us. *You're* the one who... you're the only one who's strong enough."

Elaina unloaded the panniers and brought the horse near the edge of the trail. She forgot the dizziness she'd first felt when she'd looked down at Sky's precarious position, and she talked to him, talked to the horse, talked to herself, hoping to calm all three of them.

"Are you hurt?"

"Let's figure that out later, okay? How's the plan coming?"

"I'll lead him slowly, and you'll just let him pull you up," she decided aloud as she tied a length of rope to the packsaddle.

"I'll be cut to shreds," Sky said, his voice strained. "Just make him stand. I'll get myself up."

"Hand over hand?"

"Maybe I can climb it."

Maybe he'd fall back. Maybe the horse would bolt, or the rope would break. "Maybe you should tie the end of this around you in case you . . . faint or something." She dropped the rope down to him.

"Faint! What kind of a scene are we doing here?" Reaching for the rope, he squinted up at her. There was blood running into his eye.

"One I'd like edited out," she mumbled, then turned to the horse. "You've got to be careful. You can't let him fall again."

"I'm not gonna faint," Sky informed her. "Take up the slack. Slowly."

Elaina coaxed the gray forward two steps until the rope was taut, and then she heard a groan. "Sky?" There was no answer. "Sky, are you all right?"

"I can't make it on my feet. I've gotta try hand over hand. Hold the horse steady."

Elaina held her breath. Standing by the gray's head, she couldn't watch, couldn't tell whether Sky was making progress. There was a panting gasp, another moan. "Oh, God, Elaina, get me up there. Move him!"

Elaina gauged the horse's steps, knowing Sky was being dragged over the rocks with each one. She heard him struggle against the beating he must have been taking, but she welcomed the oaths he swore as signs that he was still at the end of that rope and not on his way to the canyon floor. She looked back just as he hoisted himself over the edge with both arms and one leg, dragging the other behind him. The gray's final steps brought Sky down on his face again, but he was safe.

Lurching toward him, Elaina gasped for breath. "Sky, are you all right? My God! Your face is...and your leg. You couldn't..."

His hands were wrapped around the taut rope, his arms extended in front of him as though he were still dangling. It was his hands that stopped her questions cold. They trembled, and they bled. The rope he'd gripped as a lifeline was red with his blood.

He flinched when she touched his forearm and offered, "Let me help you take the rope off." He wasn't sure he could open his hands. He willed them to open, but at first there was only uncontrolled trembling and tightness. Hang on, he'd told himself, and he'd gone hand over hand, but his body had screamed, *No more!* and he'd had to call to her.

His hands opened slowly. He watched them and swallowed an unmanly moan, opting for a curse instead. It took a moment before he could respond to her efforts, but together they finally removed the rope from his waist. "Don't let that horse get away," he grumbled, and while she reassured herself that the lead rope was secure, Sky tried to stand. He failed.

"Sky?"

He let her prop him up. "I think I may have broken something—in my leg." Leaning heavily on her, he was able to stand without putting any weight on the injured leg. They hobbled to the high side of the trail, and she lowered him to the ground. He leaned back against a rock and took a deep breath, testing for more injuries.

"You're lucky if that's all you broke, Sky. You could have been killed."

"Lungs are working. I think the ribs are intact."

"Your head." She pushed his hair back and found an oozing cut near his hairline. "This looks bad. How far do you think we are from some kind of help?"

"You mean, besides each other?" She gave him a brave smile. "Probably a day's ride, if we had horses."

"We have *one*."

He glanced past her at the packhorse, wondering why it hadn't gone the way of the other two. "We sure do. We have one. We'll try it double."

"We also have a first-aid kit," she reminded him, and she got to her feet quickly, handing the lead rope to Sky.

"We have to get moving if we want to catch up to Rick." There was little chance of intercepting Rick's party now, and Sky realized that, but he thought it best to keep that to himself for the moment.

"That's a bad cut," Elaina repeated as she rummaged through the supply box. "And your hands are raw."

"Elaina, we have to take the essentials out of those panniers and rig up some sort of canvas sack that we can throw over the horse's withers. And we need..."

"I'll do that," she promised, returning with the first-aid box. "First things first."

He allowed her to bandage his head and clean his hands before wrapping them with gauze. It was his leg that bothered him, or, more likely, his ankle, but the pain shot the length of his left shin, and he wasn't sure where the source was. He watched her as she dabbed at his wounds, intense concern on her face. He'd tough this out for her, he told himself. She expected strong and silent; he'd give her strong and silent.

Elaina brought the supplies closer to Sky, and together they decided what was essential and how to carry it. The canvas sacks they fashioned were slung over the horse's withers, and then Sky levered himself over the animal's back and pulled Elaina up in front of him. "I do a helluva bareback mount when I've got two good legs under me," he assured her as she settled herself and got the gray moving.

"I'm sure you do." Elaina could picture it. She'd described that flying vault many times. She'd also had Swift Horse knocked from his mount once, and he'd been unconscious, sprawled with his face in the ground after a terrible blow to the head. Heroes had been injured time after time in her stories, and the heroines always took care of them. Sky's weight pressed heavily against her back, and she wondered what those women did between the fade-out after the bandaging scene in chapter nine, and the beginning of chapter ten, when the hero was already limping around.

It soon became obvious that it was asking too much of the horse to carry the weight of two people and their supplies down the rocky side of a mountain. There was no real trail, and the gray had begun to stumble occasionally. Elaina pulled him up and swung her leg over the horse's neck. Sky's arms tightened around her waist.

"I'm going to get off and walk for a while," she explained. "We have to save the horse."

"I don't want you walking. This trail gets too damn steep, and you don't like heights."

She turned and saw the hard look in Sky's eyes. The scrape above his eyebrow had turned brown-red, and the area around the bandage had swollen. There was a purpling bruise high on his left cheek. He looked as though he'd lost a fight.

"Just till we get down off this peak," she said. "I think I'd feel better walking, hugging the wall." She smiled, but he didn't. He studied her, the hardness in his eyes masking something. Elaina wondered what. "As soon as we reach a good spot, I think we should rest," she said quietly, hoping to reassure him. "We have to look out for each other now. All three of us."

Wordlessly Sky relinquished his hold, and Elaina slid to the ground. She'd planned to lead the horse, but Sky took the reins, and they moved on. She concentrated on what was ahead of her—the barren path, the rock with its red and gray striations, the occasional stand of scrub brush, the few tufts of grass. She was grateful for what was beneath her, and she tried not to see the place to her right where the ground suddenly ended.

Above her was a short blue expanse surrounded by gathering gray, with more gray encroaching on the blue all the time. Elaina watched the clouds move in, ominous, heavy, pulling the sky closer down on them. The first drops of rain stabbed her forehead. She looked up at Sky.

Sky saw nothing. He'd lost his hat in the fall, and his hair hung over his forehead, a dark, heavy curtain. He was grimacing, a pillar of pain against the gray sky, a living personification of the "End of the Trail" image, the mounted warrior slumped in defeat. He hadn't uttered a sound.

"Is it your head or your leg?" she asked.

He opened his eyes and saw the concern in hers. No sarcasm for this lady, he decided. "It's a little of each, and a lot of my pride."

"There was a little patch of grass and a few trees a ways back," she told him. "We should have climbed up there, but I was hoping for a few more trees, more shelter. Should we turn around?"

He shook his head. "I don't want to lose any ground. Let's keep going."

It was raining hard when they found shelter, a shallow excuse for a cave in a rocky outcrop, but Elaina knew she'd never seen more inviting accommodations. It was too bad the gray couldn't join them, she thought; he'd earned his keep today. But he was too big to fit, so he was tied to a rock, while Elaina unloaded the supplies and offered Sky what assistance she could. He nearly lost his grip on himself when he hit the ground, but quickly centered as much weight as he could on his good right leg. Elaina was there to bolster his left side, and together they ducked into the cave and out of the chilling rain.

They had about ten feet of depth and almost as much width, with a little water trickling down one wall. The supplies and bedrolls had been protected by a tarp they'd used as ground cover under their tent. The tent itself had been one of the nonessentials they'd left behind. Elaina unpacked quickly and wondered how she could get Sky dry without a fire. They'd have to have a fire, she decided. When the rain let up a little, she'd find some dry wood somewhere. And she'd take the gray up the trail, where she knew there was some grazing.

"But first we have to see what we can do about your..." She turned to Sky, and her stomach tightened into a hard knot. "Oh, Sky..."

He was leaning back against the cave wall, his right leg raised, his left thrown out in front of him, his expression one of agony. "Help me, Elaina. I can't get my boot off. It's too damn tight."

She went to him and tried, but the process was excruciating for both of them. He handed her his jackknife. "Cut it off. I don't think I'm going to walk out of here anyway."

"What?"

In the dim light he saw her wide-eyed expression, and he managed half a smile. "The boot, honey. Just the boot."

"Oh."

He watched her work on it and realized how patient she was, how careful. His ankle had filled the boot like poured cement, and there was no leeway for vigorous sawing. "That line about me walking out of here—I think I must have taken that right out of some script," he said as he tightened his fingers around a handy rock. "My delirium is going to be entertaining, Elaina. You'll hear one script after another."

"Are you planning on getting delirious?"

"I don't know. Isn't that the way it usually goes?" He held his breath while she slipped the remains of the boot over his heel.

She rolled his wet pants leg up and peeled his sock away. "We need cold packs."

"We have some, I think. Check the first-aid box."

When she found them under the bandages, tape and disinfectant, she wanted to kick herself. "I should have used these right away."

"*I* should have," he told her. "It *is* my leg. I forgot about them being in there. Maybe they'll still help." He was pulling his shirt off when she brought him the plastic packs, and he shot her an almost apologetic glance. "I can't handle wet clothes."

"We need a fire."

"We need a lot of things."

They looked at each other and made a silent pact to make do with what they had. His shirt was torn, and she saw that his skin was, too.

"Can you help me get my jeans off?"

"Of course."

Another look said that he wouldn't have asked, except that he couldn't manage it himself. She found a rope burn on his side and more bruises on his legs, and she didn't care what he would or wouldn't ask. He needed attention. He needed her. She applied cold packs, cleaned his wounds and applied antiseptic and bandages where she could, and helped him wrap himself in a sleeping bag.

"It looks like the rain's letting up a little," she told him. She dreaded going out there again, but the sooner she took care of the gray and located some firewood, the better. "I'll ride back to that little spot I saw, picket the horse and come back with some wood. Wouldn't a fire be nice?"

"Yeah. Real cozy." His face was tight and drawn.

"Would a cigarette help?"

"Might, if I had some, but they were in my saddlebag."

"I found some with the supplies, along with...some other stuff. Can I get you one?"

He laid his head back and came up with a thin smile. "I used to think Joe'd smell it a mile away and come running. Now I wish that were true."

She brought him a pack of Rick's brand, one Sky particularly disdained, and he watched her handle it self-consciously, like someone who had no familiarity with such things and wanted none. His hands were only scraped a little, but he kept them still while she put the end of the cigarette in his mouth and fumbled with a match. Something in him enjoyed the whole process. She held the flame steady for him, and he inhaled with a feeling of real gratitude. "You're an angel."

Hearing his own words, he glanced up through a smoky haze, immediately wishing he hadn't said them. It was such an easy expression, and it sounded too pat. She didn't belong in the company of the others whom he'd called the same thing. The hell of it was, if he'd ever known an angel, this was the lady. He wished he hadn't wasted the word on ordinary women. He wished... "I don't want you going out there in that rain, Elaina. The horse is okay for now, and we can do without a fire."

"That horse deserves to be put out to stud in a field of clover," Elaina declared as she watched Sky relish his cigarette. "I can't let him stand out there tied to a rock. He could easily have run off with the others, you know."

"You haven't eaten anything."

"We'll eat when I get back."

He took another long pull on his cigarette and looked away from her. "You get back here pronto, or I'll be out there looking for you. I don't like being alone in the dark." He figured it was one of the biggest lies he'd ever told, which was probably why she was giggling.

"*Pronto?* You do need a new scriptwriter, Mr. Hunter. Your lines are dated."

"Well...like I said..." He stared at the burning end of his cigarette. "I need a lot of things. You just get back here."

She didn't want to leave him, and she wanted to be back with him even before she left. The gray wasn't sure he wanted to go anywhere, either, but Elaina coaxed him to carry her to the small patch of grass she was glad she'd passed by earlier. In this rain, they needed better shelter. She strung a picket line and staked the horse to it with a loop just above his front hoof, leaving him plenty of slack to graze. A flash of lightning cut the dark evening sky in half, and she was glad she wasn't riding the gray when the crack of thunder followed. She saw that he stood his ground, but he was getting nervous.

Elaina still needed wood. A deadfall provided some dry pieces, and she rolled them up in the tarp she'd brought with her. "Take all you can carry," she told herself. The sound of her voice was somehow comforting, but the wind's voice carried more power. It rattled the pines and shook the grass. Elaina reassured herself that the picket line was secure, then headed toward the cave.

Her left hand kept her in constant physical touch with the rocky mountain wall. She felt too close to the dark sky, too near to the lightning, too harassed by the thunder. Darkness closed in on her, and the air grew heavier. It was going to rain again, probably harder this time. With each flash of lightning she imagined evil spirits looking for her, scheming to knock her off the mountain. Elaina clutched her parcel of wood under her arm and held fast, picking her way down the slope. Let them try to loosen her hold, she told herself. She was steadfast. She would move slowly and carefully, but she would get there eventually.

The lightning redoubled its efforts, lacing itself through slate-gray clouds in erratic patterns. Thunder made the whole mountain tremble, and Elaina knew she'd climbed too high this time. This was a place for wild things and mythical creatures, not for city girls. The path was too narrow, too rocky and too steep. A deafening crash pasted her to the wall, and there she stood for several moments, eyes tightly closed.

"You'll make it," she told herself aloud, and she took a step. "You will make it." Another step was possible. Clutching at the rocks with one hand and the parcel of wood with the other, she took one step at a time until she reached the cave.

She'd hardly been aware of the pelting rain, but when she ducked into the cave, she knew she was drenched. Sky was propped up in the shadows, eyes closed, and Elaina thought as she set her bundle down that sleep was a blessing for him. Then he raised his hand to his mouth and produced a red glow at the end of a cigarette.

"Find a little mountaintop resort up there, did you?" He exhaled the last of the smoke from his lungs. "Thought maybe you ran into someone you knew and forgot the time."

"I found some dry wood." She had a piece of it in her hand, and she extended it toward him like an offering.

"And I just found the 'other stuff' in with the supplies." He lifted a pint flask in a salute to her return. "Medicinal Everclear. Rick thought of everything."

"I take it that's not on the inventory."

"It's not on Joe's usual inventory, so I guess somebody up there likes me." He tasted his find, then cursed it. "I hate this stuff."

"Did the ice packs help at all?" she asked quietly.

"Some." Not a hell of a lot. Not when his head pounded with images of her. Not when he heard the thunder and saw the world turn upside down for her as it had for him.

"If I put the fire over here, the draft should take the smoke, and this wall should protect the—"

"Where have you been?"

She looked at him curiously. Was Sky actually capable of asking such a stupid question? "I found a pile of wood that was pretty well protected; I think it's almost completely—"

"What took you so damn long?" He spoke in crisp, quiet, evenly spaced syllables.

"What took me so long?" Elaina's throat tightened as her back grew stiff. "What *took* me so long?

Do you have any idea...*any* idea how...how..." Her voice cracked, and she took a deep breath and half whispered, "How high up we are?"

He allowed himself a slow sigh. "Yeah."

"How low that sky is out there?"

"How low this Sky is in here," he mumbled, crushing his cigarette in the little hollow he'd made next to him. He had finished half the pack.

"I went to get wood," she reminded him in a raspy voice.

"I know."

"And to find some grass for the only means of transportation we have."

"I know that."

"I'm sorry I was a little late getting home, but I ran into some bad weather," she continued acidly. "It's a wonder you didn't—"

"I did." He took a quick swig from the flask, then dropped his head back against the rocky wall. "I tried, anyway. I can't walk on it at all, Elaina. I blacked out."

She settled back on her heels and fought for control. No tears, she told herself. He didn't need that, and neither did she. She busied herself with making the fire and facing facts. "It's broken, then, isn't it?"

"Probably. I don't know what a broken leg's supposed to feel like."

"It's supposed to hurt." She watched one of the pine cones burst into flames under her little pile of wood.

"Then we've got one of the symptoms." He studied the flask, considered, then took another swallow. It tasted like something he might use to dissolve rust. "I don't drink," he said bleakly.

"You need something for the pain, and that's all we've got." Satisfied with her fire, she brushed her hands on her wet jeans and rose to her feet, ducking to keep from hitting her head on the low ceiling. Already the warmth felt good.

"I need a lot of things." He knew he'd said it before, and it sounded as lame as he was. Elaina glanced sideways and caught the hard edge of pain in his eyes. She turned to him and let him absorb her sympathy. "Come over here, Elaina."

He took her hand as soon as he could reach it. It was as if he'd been waiting forever just to do that. "You had me worried, you know. That's why I barked at you when you came in." The mountain seemed to rumble, and then a sharp crack split the air. "You know how that sounded to me, knowing you were out there?" His voice was soft, soothing after the thunderclap.

The opening of the cave brightened with a flash of lightning, and she said, "Do you know how that looks from out there on that ledge?"

The heavens rumbled again as he brought her palm to his lips. It smelled of pine pitch, but he tasted blood. "What's this?" he asked, squinting at the raw outside edge of her hand. "What happened?" But the remembered terror in her eyes told him everything.

She'd made her way back here on prayers—her own, no doubt, and his, too, the first one he'd said in as long as he could remember.

"I was scared," she whispered.

He hooked his arm over her head and pulled it against his bare chest with a sigh. "So was I. I never felt so damned helpless in my life."

Another flash of lightning drove her closer, and he held her tight. "We're safe in here," she murmured. "It feels so good to be safe."

"And warm. God, I've been chilled to the marrow." He rubbed his palm over her back. "This is all you've got to wear, isn't it? You've got to get dry."

His skin felt warm, Elaina realized, almost unnaturally so. She sat up, touched his face and found it to be clammy. "You're not feverish, are you?"

"I needed this fire," he said with a wan smile. "It feels like California sun."

"You need something to eat."

"I'll eat if you'll take your clothes off."

"That's the most shameless bribery I've ever heard." She smiled and unbuttoned her blouse. "But I hate wet cloth."

"It looks damn good on you, but then—" he let his head drop back, closed his eyes and sighed. "—everything does."

"I'm keeping my underwear on."

"Good. I've had these delicious fantasies about hiring a cook who works like that in the kitchen. Who won't wear anything else."

"Do you have a cook?" It was a struggle to pull off her wet boots.

"Haven't found one yet."

Wet jeans were worse. "I wonder why."

"The employment agency has no imagination. I think I ought to reword the requirements. Tell 'em I'm looking for a romance writer who moonlights as a cook." Opening his eyes to the sound of her rummaging through the supply sack, he smiled at her back. Plain white bra and panties. He'd never seen prettier. "Or vice versa. Want a job?"

"We might have to compromise on the fantasies," she told him as she pulled a plastic egg case and a can of Spam from the sack. "I have quite a few of my own."

"Well, don't confuse the issue while mine are coming true." Keep talking to me, he thought as he took another sip of bitter fire. Keep me thinking about something other than the fact that somebody's shooting arrows into my leg.

"You need to put something else into your stomach before you drink any more of that stuff, or you'll be fantasizing about snakes."

"Rats," he told her, infusing the word with a tone of utter disgust. "A room full of rats. That's my worst nightmare. But I won't get it from a pint of Everclear." He held the flask up and weighed its power in ounces. "All I'll get out of this is one good drunk, maybe one and a half."

"Or one good headache, maybe one and a half."

"The ominous voice of good sense." The eggs smelled good, so he set the flask aside and hoped he wouldn't need it anymore. He would concentrate on the sound of her voice and the way she looked with the firelight glinting in her golden hair. "Did you know it was female?" he asked her. He was on the verge of being serious about something that made little sense, and he gave the alcohol credit for its fast work. "Good sense is female. The Greeks had it figured that wisdom was a woman, a goddess."

"Ancient Greek women had very few rights," Elaina pointed out as she flipped an egg and a slice of Spam. "How do you explain that?"

"The men were scared. They knew what would happen. Give women a few rights and, before you know it, you can't keep 'em in the kitchen. They want to be up in the mountains frying eggs in their underwear."

Elaina took a peek into the pan. "I've got news for you. These eggs are stark naked."

She made him laugh, and for a few seconds the pain fled. He would be able to eat as long as she kept talking to him. He watched her move about their hideaway, finding places to spread their clothes to dry, adding wood to the fire, bringing in rainwater and washing everything, including herself. Then she took out the first-aid box.

"Bring that over here, Elaina."

She glanced at him, holding up her injured hand. "I was going to, but first I thought I'd . . ."

"Please. Bring them to me."

The box and her wound. She knew what he meant, and she complied. "I had it in mind to take care of you, Elaina. All along, that's the way I pictured it." He took the box and ministered to the raw places on the side of her hand with delicate tenderness. "I wanted to take you to the most beautiful place I knew, provide food for you and give you pleasure and make you think I was one hell of a man."

"But only for a few days," she reminded him.

"I tried promising forever once. Forever isn't as long as it sounds." She flinched when he applied the antiseptic, and he blew on her hand as he remembered his mother had once done for him. "Maybe I can only be one hell of a man for a few days. I'm an actor."

"I think I can tell when you're acting and when you're not, Sky. When you're acting, you're a hell of an actor. When you're not . . ." She touched his cheek with her injured hand, and he looked up at her. "Let me see your leg."

"I don't want you to see it," he said stubbornly. "I don't want to see it, either."

They both looked at the lower end of the sleeping bag, where he'd hoped to hide the fact that his left leg—foot, ankle and much of the calf and shin—had become a formless piece of bloat. She moved to uncover him, and he made no move to stop her.

"It should be elevated, I think."

He reached for the flask again. "Probably."

"Did you use all the cold packs?"

"There might be more."

"I'll look." She found a few. Insisting that he lie flat on his back, she used canvas and the folded tarp to prop his leg as high as she could. "You always see broken legs suspended from those hospital contraptions," she told him as she arranged the cold packs. "This must be what the doctor would order. Maybe a few aspirin would help you sleep."

"Forget the aspirin, honey; I've decided to get very, very drunk." He didn't like the silence that followed, so he added, "Aspirin can cause problems with bleeding."

Moving to the head of his improvised bed, she watched him take a drink from his flask. "Between the two of us, we might have enough medical knowledge to make a living selling Egyptian snake oil elixir." A trickle of the drink rolled down his chin when he tipped the flask up, and Elaina caught the drop on her thumb and tasted it. "I take it you haven't always been a teetotaler."

"No, I haven't," he confessed. "I don't like to quit when I get started. When I start to talk your ear off, it's time to take the bottle away."

"And then you'll be able to sleep?"

"God, I hope so." Elaina sized up the sleeping arrangements and decided that there would be room for her next to him when and if the drugging effect of the alcohol took control of his pain. He could see what she was thinking, and he smiled. "I'll be harmless, and you'll be warm. Just do me one more favor, Elaina."

"What's that?"

"When I do start talking your ear off, don't take any notes."

Reluctantly, she promised.

Chapter Eight

The cat retracted its claws. The gut-gouging pain subsided, becoming just a small annoyance that could be ignored with a little effort. Sky's ex-wife, an even smaller annoyance, floated down the river of his mind, and he laughed aloud.

"Things must be looking up," Elaina remarked, busying herself with the dried food in the pack. She'd just found some beans, which probably would have become an authentic Western trail supper in Rick's Dutch oven. Elaina decided to soak them and give them a try over her fire.

"Why? What did you find?" Sky propped himself up on his elbow to get a better view, though he was more interested in Elaina than in whatever was keeping her so busy. Unfortunately, her shirt had dried quickly, and she was wearing it again.

"Beans. Do you know anything about cooking beans?"

"Yeah. Soak, boil and add anything you can find to make them taste like something besides beans. And talk to me while you're at it." He searched his mind for a provocative springboard. "Why aren't you married, Elaina?"

Her hands stilled over her work. "I thought we'd been over that already."

"We've been over the fact that I'm no longer married. We haven't really talked about you much, Miss Delacourte, the writer. Who are you, anyway?"

She covered the beans and set them aside, choosing her answer as she did. "I'm a woman you met in a bar."

"Uh-uh, lady, that won't do. That doesn't say anything about you. It was a fluke, your being at Shorty's that night. You looked like a butterfly hanging around the garbage dump." He grinned, pleased with his wit.

"I'm not married because I don't have a husband, and you promised to lie flat on your back."

"In return for the privilege of getting drunk, as I remember." He sipped at his anesthetic and complied. The liquor was working. For all he knew, the elevation of his leg and the cold packs might have been working, too. The dull throb in his ankle had become bearable, and he felt like talking. "You're the right kind of woman for a man who's looking for a wife. Why haven't you taken a husband, Elaina?''

Elaina said nothing. She'd wanted to sit beside him, hold his hand and talk nonsense with him until he fell asleep. Nonsense, not sore spots.

"You said you'd never been married," he reminded her, pressing.

"The law says I haven't been married." The pot of beans held her gaze. "Once, when I was very young and pregnant, I thought I was married. Then I lost the baby, and our parents had the marriage annulled."

"How old were you?" he asked quietly.

"Sixteen."

"And you had a miscarriage?"

She nodded, feeling the loss again as she did each time the memory returned. She remembered how soon after the first loss the second one had come. "He was eighteen, and the most beautiful boy I'd ever known. They packed him off to college, and that was that." Shaking off the sorrow, she glanced up quickly. "How's that for a happy ending?"

He was listening closely, watching her with eyes like soft chocolate. "You don't strike me as the kind of writer who'd use that for an ending. Your fans wouldn't tolerate it."

"Well, it *was* the end—" his eyes unnerved her, and she glanced away quickly, nearly losing the words "—of something."

"Come over here, Elaina, and tell me what ended."

"You should sleep," she suggested gently, but she went over and sat beside him on a small piece of their combined bedrolls.

"I will, pretty soon now." He saw that her hands were clasped tightly over her upraised knees, and he took one of them in his and soothed her knuckles with his thumb. "Do you miss this husband who wasn't a husband?"

"I hardly remember what he looked like," she answered in a small, tight voice.

"But you miss the child you might have had."

"Sometimes."

They watched the fire she'd been careful to tend with bits of precious fuel. The rain fell steadily, splashing over the rocks outside the shelter. There was something in the combined sounds, the crackle and the splash, that made Elaina feel warm sitting where she was.

"Funny," Sky reflected as he crooked his arm beneath his head. "I was number six in a family of ten kids. We never had enough of anything, and I swore I'd never..." With Elaina's hand feeling warm and small in his, those oaths he'd sworn seemed hollow, and he lacked the will even to repeat them. "I married a woman who wanted babies, and I refused to give her any. She went looking for someone who would, while I went off to seek fame, fortune and the company of women who wanted nothing but good times."

"What did you find?"

He searched the rocky ceiling. "A little fame, a little fortune and a long parade of..." The rise and fall of his brow was quick dismissal. "Some women don't need children. You buy a few drinks, you go somewhere, you take care of your immediate needs. No demands, no questions, no promises. No hearth and home."

Elaina kept her eyes on the fire. Her memory of Sky's lovemaking danced in her head, and she couldn't look at anything but the fire. We made love, she insisted silently. We made *love*.

Sky's chuckle made her stiffen. "Hearth and home, Elaina. Look at this, will you? A cave and a camp fire, and you provided both. That should have been my job."

She looked down at him and saw vague regret in his eyes. "Why?"

"Because I was your trusted Indian guide." He smiled, the regret lingering before he wiped it away with a sip from the flask.

"That stuff must taste awful." He offered her a sip with a silent gesture, but she shook her head. "For medicinal purposes, it's all yours."

"It tastes like fuel oil at first, but after a while it goes down easy." He lifted the metal flask again and eyed it suspiciously. "Too easy."

"Are you drunk yet?"

"Pretty close." He capped the bottle and handed it to her. "Closer than I ever wanted to be again. I don't like the feeling."

"It's better than pain, isn't it?"

He laughed, enjoying the nearness of her. She was as innocent as rainwater, and she was real—as real as the pain he'd felt before the liquor had dulled his own sense of reality. His skin felt rubberized and his head was slightly awash, and he wasn't real himself at the moment, but she was. He needed that.

"Not necessarily," he told her. "Pain keeps everything in perspective."

"Like broken bones?"

"If it's broken you need to know it's broken so you can get it fixed. Some people want to deaden everything. Feeling no pain means you don't feel anything at all. Zombies," he said solemnly. "The world's full of walking dead."

"You sound like the voice of experience."

"I've known a few zombies," he admitted, and the thought made him pass his free hand over his bare chest as he tried to measure the degree to which he'd numbed himself. He decided he was still there. "People's souls can be devoured by their habits, and pretty soon you look in their eyes and all you can see is vacancy. I saw that look in the mirror once. Scared the hell out of me."

"What did you do?"

"Broke every mirror in the house and changed my ways," he said lightly.

She smiled at the thought of what must have been a terrible rampage, if he was telling her the truth. She imagined that Hollywood houses were full of mirrors. "What an awful mess."

"I didn't replace a one of them, either, till I'd rejoined the living. You can't put anything over on a mirror."

"No, I suppose not."

"You're like that, too." He raised his hand from his chest to her chin and turned her face toward him. "You're an observer. Nothing escapes those pretty blue eyes, those delicate ears." He touched her temple near the corner of her eye, then traced the curve of her ear with one finger. "Mirrors don't make any judgments about what they see, Elaina. Do you? Do you hate seeing me like this?"

"I hate seeing you in pain," she said, drawn to the softness in his eyes.

"I want to see you again after we get out of this mess. But only on good days, huh? Not when there's pain." He smiled gently, touching his thumb to the middle of her lower lip.

"I didn't mean that I wouldn't . . . I meant that it hurts me to see you hurt like this. If the alcohol helps . . ."

"Sometimes it helps. If you hurt for me, it means you can feel, and that's good. I ran away from the reservation because I didn't want to hurt for anybody else. Worse, I didn't even want to hurt for me." It was good to touch her, he told himself. She grounded him. She kept him from drifting away. Her cheek was soft, warm. There was so much he wanted to tell her all of a sudden.

"Your parents lived on the reservation?" He gave a single nod. "So you came out here to stay with your uncle?"

"Summers mostly, until I got older. I married my high school sweetheart and found out high school sweethearts don't make the best wives, not for people who don't like who they were in high school and are looking for a way to be somebody else."

"You found a way to be lots of other people," she reflected for him. "How did you become an actor?"

"I came out to Silver Moon one summer to work, and there was a film crew out here on location. I got a job as an extra, and I got hooked. You're right." He smiled up at her. "I liked playing at being lots of other people. But once I stopped running away from being myself, I realized that acting was a craft, not a game. I study it. I work hard at it, and I know what I could be doing, what I'm capable of doing." He stretched his arm toward the ceiling, fingers splayed as he watched his own gesture. "God, I can almost reach it, but not quite. Not quite." He drew his hand back slowly, bringing with it a fistful of air.

"It's frustrating when you know you're ready for another challenge and the opportunity seems just out of reach. The time seems right for you to hold out for more, doesn't it?" she asked.

"It does," he said, and he liked the feeling the words gave him. "It damn sure does." She shifted her position, and it brought her a bit closer. He looked up at her again, and though she looked a little hazy, he could see her better than he had before. "You've got some of those feelings, too, haven't you? Frustration? Ambition? Just plain hunger?"

"Yes, of course I do," she told him. "I think everybody—"

"No, not everybody. Just you and me." His voice came softly. "Let's just talk about you and me. I want you, too. I think I want you as much as I want that dream I've been chasing."

"Maybe that's because I'm here, and the dream is hundreds of miles away."

"It's because you're here, and I see you. I see how good you are." She laughed, and he knew he must have sounded drunk, the kind of overly serious drunk that amused the sober. He guessed he *was* drunk, then, and he knew he was cold and miserable and tired. Elaina was like his other dreams, a little beyond his grasp at the moment. "Okay, so my lines are coming off a little spongy. Will you sleep with me anyway?"

"Now you're getting pretty direct," she said, still smiling.

"I just want you to hold me and keep me warm after the fire goes out." He lifted enough of the bedroll to reveal the length of his side. "And I'll return the favor."

Elaina went to him and did as he asked. His strong right thigh felt like a Yule log against her legs, and the added warmth she found as she nestled in the crook of his arm made the fire unnecessary. She worried that she was the one unable to return the favor when he shivered and pulled her closer as he slept. He rested fitfully, trying to move his left leg at times and groaning in his sleep when the attempt proved painful. Elaina dozed off now and then, but she was alert each time he moved.

She'd slept with every hero she'd created, but she had never slept with men. There had been one boy, one beautiful boy, who'd become a legend of innocence in Elaina's mind. Their love had been pure and ill-fated. The heroes who'd replaced him had been pure, too, each in his own way. They'd been carved in stone, each one strong and bold, and each one free of the doubts that had made the legendary boy less than perfect. Her heroes always controlled every situation. But Elaina created their situations for them, and, in the end, she was in control. She made everything work out, and her heroines were the benefactors.

Now she slept with a man she'd had no part in creating. The fact that she couldn't direct his mind and his actions gave her a helpless feeling. She knew what a hero meant when he said he wanted a woman, but what did a man mean? What did *this* man mean? She couldn't mold him, or direct his action. If she allowed herself to love him, that meant loving the man he was, and she'd already felt confused and disappointed by some of his behavior. He'd made love to her one night, then withdrawn the following morning. He hadn't said all the things she'd expected, hadn't told her that their night of lovemaking had changed his life and that now he would change hers.

He was a man who knew how to play a role, and that was a fact she could not allow herself to forget. He was also a man who made her feel the depth of her womanhood, and that was a gift she would always remember with joy.

"Damn cold mountain rain. It's summer, for God's sake; where's the sun?"

The grumbler leaned on both elbows, propping himself up for his fourth curse of the morning as he scowled at the bone-chilling drizzle. The blackest clouds, however, were in Sky's face, and the worst storm was in his head.

"I think it's gone to California for a while." The scowl was turned on Elaina, but she smiled it down bravely. "The sun, I mean. I understood California's the place to be for that."

"Funny girl." He eased himself down on his back and sighed. "Lemme try some more aspirin."

"It's not time for more aspirin. How about more coffee?"

"The last time I had to get up and go outside, we had a major production here," he reminded her. "For the sake of my pride, I'll forgo the coffee. Damn, we've gotta get out of here, Elaina."

"We will, as soon as the rain stops."

"I'll be crazy by then."

"No, you won't."

"My whole back feels like hamburger."

"I've been studying our quarters here, and I think I've figured out a way to elevate your leg without using all that other stuff. We need to put the canvas under you, along with anything else we can find to cushion you. Your back . . . What's so funny?"

"Can I put any soft thing I can find underneath me?" It felt good to laugh, even at himself. She gave him a mock hard look and he shrugged.

"I think I have an interesting sort of a south-of-the-border egg and refried bean breakfast going here," she told him, gesturing toward the coals in her firepit. "After we eat I'll have to find more wood."

Sky pitched his voice low. "Elaina, you are not to set foot out of this cave without my permission. It's raining."

Lifting a pan from the coals, she sang, "It's raining. It's pouring. The old man is snoring."

"You're being insolent. Permission is denied." Then, in his own voice, he wondered, "Did I snore last night? I didn't, did I?"

"Such vanity," she tossed back with a teasing smile. "What if you did?"

"Dead drunk and flat on my back, I probably did. God, this is the most inept play I've ever made for a woman."

"Am I the first one you've dragged into a cave?"

"You're having a convenient lapse of memory, honey. I distinctly remember *you* dragging *me* into this cave."

"Would that it had been otherwise," she sighed wistfully as she dished up their plates. "What a story."

"I'm sure I would have had great dialogue." A plate of beans and eggs appeared under his nose, and his stomach protested. "Ugh!"

"Oh, come on, Sky, my dialogue isn't that bad."

"No, I mean this stuff," he groaned, pushing the plate away.

"My cooking isn't that bad, either."

"Yeah, but my hangover is. You wouldn't be able to drag me outside quick enough if I tried to eat that now."

"You're sure?" He nodded. "If I heat it up again later, will you try?"

"I'll try. Later."

She set his plate aside and sat near him with a plate for herself, glancing at him over her first forkful. He looked jaundiced. She gave him a pleasant smile and moved several feet away.

"Thanks."

"It's really not bad," she told him. "In fact, I think I'm getting pretty good at this camp-fire cooking. Did you see how I used that thing from your tackle box for a grate?" He groaned. "Well, I had to improvise. I'm finding that if I tried to cook the way I described it in my books, I'd burn everything. The only camp cooking I've ever done was over a Coleman stove."

"We may be stuck here for another day."

"It isn't raining very hard now," she offered hopefully.

"I know, but it's overcast, and the ground out there is slick as a cat's...paws. And we're riding double and bareback."

Elaina giggled. "Slick as a cat's *paws*?"

"I'm trying to be nice."

"And you *are* nice."

After finishing her beans she picked up his plate, scraped the contents back into the pot and set the plates aside while she continued to praise him. "For a man with a terrible hangover, I think you're doing very well in that department. I'd like to take one little peek at your leg before I go out shopping for firewood."

"I'll let you take a peek at anything else," he said flatly. "The leg isn't going on display."

She came to his side, her face full of sympathy. "It's bad, huh?"

"Bad enough."

"Has it swollen any more, do you think?"

"No. I think it's gone down some."

"Then why...?"

"I don't like having you look at me like that, Elaina. I'm a man. I don't like pity."

"I'm a woman," she said softly. "I don't know pity. I just know...caring. Flat on your back, you're still a man, Sky."

"I'm the one who should be taking care of you up here in these mountains," he insisted. "I don't want you going out there again. You're going out to do something I should be doing."

"Indian women always gathered the wood," she reminded him with a smile.

"You're not an Indian woman. You're a dude, a guest. You came straight from the city, and this was all supposed to be staged. A controlled demonstration of surviving in the wilderness. Damn it, Elaina, you're too..." He closed his eyes, furrowing his brow in a gesture that could have meant pain or concern or frustration. "I don't like it when you're gone," he said firmly.

"I've only been gone once. And I got back okay."

He opened his eyes, and the look in them told her that he remembered it as a bad time.

"That was during a thunderstorm," she added. "It'll take me half that time this morning. Less than that. We need a fire."

He caught her hand before she could rise to her feet. "I need...maybe just a kiss."

She leaned over him, and he drew her head down. His lips were dry, and she moistened them for him. Even after she'd kissed him and he'd kissed her back, she wasn't satisfied. He was at her mercy, and she'd have a minute more, just to touch him. She pressed her cheek to his, hoping the gesture wouldn't embarrass him.

He tightened his arms around her and sighed. "Oh, Elaina, I'm sorry about all this."

"I'm sorry you're hurt, Sky. But I'm glad I came with you. I'm glad we're together."

"Don't be crazy, girl. We're in a lot of trouble."

"But we'll be all right," she promised, drawing away. "We'll be fine."

Elaina beat down her fears and made quick work of finding firewood. She managed to give the packhorse some water and to move the picket line so he could have fresh grazing, but she was in such a hurry that she fumbled with each knot. Sky was worried about her. She kind of liked that idea, but she didn't want to wring too much out of it. He was stuck on a mountain with a broken leg, and she, dude that she was, was all he had. It was important to her to be able to return with dry wood and a report that she had taken care of the horse.

Sky was waiting for her, again with the cigarette in his mouth, but his mood was somewhat improved. "That was quick," he offered with a welcoming smile.

She didn't tell him that she'd practically run part of the way back. "It's not so bad when there's more light and that thunder isn't crashing all around you."

"Any sign of clearing?"

"The clouds seem to be moving around up there." He needed some kind of reassurance. He needed to be made more comfortable, and she wasn't sure her plan would work, but the time had come to try. "How's the hangover?"

"I think I'm winning that battle," he reported. "I think I could eat some of your refried beans if you want to re-refry them."

"I'll do that as soon as I get you resituated. We're going to get that swelling to go down, and we're going to make you a more comfortable bed."

He watched her work out her plan, putting every piece of tarp and canvas they had under the bedroll and rigging up a sling by stringing rope around a boulder here and through a crevice there. He smoked another cigarette while she fashioned a padded shelf for his leg in the rope sling. By the time she motioned for him to try it, his leg was throbbing, ready to be hung like a slab of meat in a butcher's locker.

"How's that?"

"Great. Your imagination serves us well."

"How's the bed? I tried to get rid of all the gravel."

"Much better. Almost as good as a water bed."

"Oh, I wish we had a water bed up here. Wouldn't that be great?"

"We've got enough water for one." He stubbed out his cigarette and looked at her longingly. A real bed would have felt fine right about then if he could have shared it with her. She looked tired, and her jeans were soaked again. Her hair hung from the crown of her head like twisted swathes of wheat. She hadn't taken time for her hair or her clothes, and now she was turning to rekindle the fire and take care of his food. His heart ached to give her a proper bed.

"Take a break now, Elaina. I'm not that hungry."

"This will only take a minute. You need to eat before we both take a rest."

She flashed him a shy look, and he knew that she would share this bed, the only one they had. He waited quietly and ate without a word, doing that much for her. She needed his strength, whatever he could muster of it. She'd never be able to get them down off this mountain, he thought. He was the man. It was for him to do.

"Do you have a hairbrush?" he asked as he watched her peel her damp jeans off her legs.

"No." Her hands flew to her hair the way a woman's will when she suspects she's been caught looking like a man's worst nightmare. "I guess I look like a cavewoman."

He smiled. "You look like an angel, Elaina. One who just braved the elements to get back to me. There's a comb in my back pocket."

She put her jeans near the fire and searched through his, coming up with a small black comb. "Bring it to me, please," he said. "Let me do something for you."

It was a lot of hair for such a small comb, but he worked section by section, gently easing the tangles out. They talked about his films and her books, laughed at things that at one time they'd thought too important to their careers to be funny. They confided in one another easily, as though they'd been friends for years. Nothing seemed too absurd or sacred to be told as he performed the personal task of combing her hair.

"I've been writing what people want me to write," she confessed. "What people want to read. What I want to dream about."

"You dream about ol' Fast Horse, do you?"

"Sometimes."

"What do you dream, Elaina?" He said her name slowly, listening to the feminine sound of it. He liked to call her by name.

"Oh, I dream of being captured and rescued and cared for, and wanted, by a strong and gentle man."

"And that's what Fast Horse is? A strong and gentle man?"

"Basically, yes. A woman's man, I guess."

"He oughta be. A woman made him. Does he ever fall short of your expectations, maybe slip a little...make a mistake?"

"Only small ones. He shows his temper sometimes, maybe broods a little."

"I brood a lot," he admitted, running his fingers through the waves in her hair. The tangles were gone; he just wanted to feel the corn silk. "I've been taking care of number one for a long time. I don't suppose Fast Horse is ever selfish or vain."

"No, of course not." She turned to give him a curious smile. "Why the interest in someone who's made of paper and ink?"

"I'm a little concerned about how someone who's made of flesh and blood is supposed to live up to these stereotypes of yours. I'm having enough trouble with the celluloid kind."

"You needn't worry," she told him, laying her hand over his chest. "Stereotypes don't live at all, except in people's minds. They don't breathe. No heart pumps ink."

"I want you to dream about me."

"I have," she said honestly.

"I'd like for you to believe that I'm always strong and gentle, unselfish, brave, all those good things, but it's not true. If I were eighteen years old and somebody put a lot of pressure on me, I might run, too."

"You're not eighteen years old," she said, telling herself that she wasn't sixteen anymore, either.

"No, but I was once. An eighteen-year-old boy is about as romantic as a young stud at breeding time." He smiled briefly. "Or an actor with a broken leg. I want you to dream about me, Elaina, but I'm no more like Fast Horse than your young husband was."

"Why should I dream about you, then?" she asked, turning toward him because she had her own answer already.

"Because it's raining all around us, Elaina. It's probably raining in California, too. But we've got shelter for each other. We've got warmth, and we've got . . ."

His kiss was hot, and his tongue burned sweetly on her lips. Her closeness made it difficult, but he managed to wedge his hand between them to unbutton her blouse and find her breast. They both sighed at the discovery.

"What can I do?" she whispered desperately.

"Touch me," he rasped near her ear. "Let me touch you."

"It won't be enough."

"We'll make it enough."

He could have been satisfied just to touch and be touched. When she put her hand on him, he felt cherished, and he reached down to cherish her. His mind spun away from his pain and dallied with ecstasy. And then he heard his name, high-pitched with her need, and he knew she was right. It wasn't enough.

"Move over me, honey. Ride me. Let me set you free."

"Sky?"

"It's okay. I'm taking my leg down, just for a minute."

"I don't want you to..."

"I won't," he promised, lifting her hips as she straddled him. "I'll be careful."

"I mean hurt yourself. I don't want you to...oh, Sky...don't hurt yourself."

"I won't. Don't be shy now."

"Oh! Oh, my beautiful...beautiful...Sky..."

"That's right, Elaina. Beautiful Sky. Make lightning, honey. Make thunder. Make it...rain."

"It's so good...."

"Yes," he whispered, and felt the richness of her pleasure. "Yes," he promised as he took himself from her quickly and held her close. "I'll take care of you."

"I want rain...inside me, Sky."

Her voice was a soft plea, a sated, sleepy half dream. He pressed his lips against her temple. "And I want to make something grow inside you, Elaina. God help me, I do."

Chapter Nine

A thousand angry muscles rebelled inside Sky when he woke. He ached everywhere, and every muscle he flexed screamed at him for his audacity. He'd slept with his left leg in Elaina's contraption, and he had to admit that keeping it up had helped to control the swelling, which seemed to have localized in his ankle.

Elaina stirred in the little pocket she'd made for herself at his side. Twisting against the constriction of his sling, Sky turned as he reached to pull her closer, and she filled his arms like warm, soft wax poured into his mold. She sighed and snuggled against him, and he found himself smiling broadly at the far wall. He had a broken ankle, but he felt pretty damn good.

A downy blanket of contentment settled over him, a sense of genuine well-being, and it came to him that Elaina had not created it for him. It was actually his feeling, emanating from somewhere within himself. It had not been seduced, induced or reduced to some common denominator of sameness. He'd made his own contentment with his own affection, strongly felt and freely given. He felt it now as he watched her sleep, and he knew that he would feel it when he watched her brush her teeth, or put his next meal over the fire, or snap his picture while he squinted into the sun. He decided that he was hooked, and he chuckled aloud.

"Mmm, you're laughing at me." Elaina kept her eyes closed, letting the sound of his amusement and the smooth warmth of his skin sensitize her to being awake. "I must be sleeping funny."

"Actually I'm the one who slept funny," he told her, smiling as he brushed a strand of hair from her forehead with a single finger. "I've got the aches and pains to prove it."

"How's your main pain?" she murmured.

"You tell me. You feeling all right?"

She smiled back, her eyes still closed. "Never better." She kissed his chest, the part of him nearest her mouth, and finally opened her eyes to allow herself the pleasure of being caught up in the warmth of his gaze. "Never, *ever* any better. Am I really your main pain?"

She looked sleepy-eyed sweet, and he wanted to tell her that she could be. He wanted to confess that if she denied him access to her heart he would hurt badly, but he decided to return the smile and be charming instead of honest. "Hardly," he assured her. "It's not as bad as it was."

"I wish we had more cold packs." She stretched, and the friction she created between their bodies made him groan. Her smile told him there was nothing unintentional about the movement.

"As long as we're wishing, how about a Jacuzzi and a king-size bed?"

"How about a doctor and an X-ray lab?" she added sensibly, propping herself up on her elbow.

"They'll get me sooner or later. I'm looking for comforts."

"Comforts?" She told herself not to tease, but she was in a teasing mood. "We came out here to rough it. We wanted to suffer and sacrifice and get in touch with ourselves."

He snapped his fingers. "Damn, I forgot my hair shirt."

"Hair shirt? Is that traditional? I know about the Ghost Dance shirts, and the warrior society shirts, but I don't remember any..." Tapping her thumbnail against her teeth, she made a show of considering her mental files.

"It's a recently acquired form of self-torture," he instructed. "A shirt made from the hair of the sheep. Worn directly against the skin, it causes subtle but sublime torture."

"You have an allergy to wool?"

"Exactly." He took the hand that was poised near her lips and placed it in the middle of his chest. "My skin's very sensitive. I have to be careful what I put next to it."

"Flannel and denim become you."

"In public, maybe. In the privacy of my cave, I prefer soft hands." With the back of his hand he touched the underside of her breast and watched her catch her lower lip between her teeth. "How about you?"

"Gentle hands," she specified, her hand stirring over him.

"Mmmm, yes. Let's add a shower to our list of wishes. I'd love to work up a lather over you right about now."

In the next few quiet seconds the sound of steady rain moved from background music to the center of their attention. Sky was the first to quirk a suggestive brow.

"It'll be cold," Elaina said.

"I doubt if that'll matter. I'm pretty well heated up myself. Do we have any soap?"

She nodded. "I'll stoke up the fire. Can you stand on that leg?"

"With a little help from my friend."

"I do have something for you," she said, pushing herself up to sit on her hip. "I hope it's strong enough. I didn't believe it when I saw it just lying there, the perfect shape. I didn't even have to cut it."

Judging from the light in her eyes, she could well have a magic carpet parked right outside the cave door, he thought. She sat up proudly, her legs covered by the sleeping bag, her breasts pale. He remembered the statue of "The Little Mermaid," and he dreaded the moment when she would free her feet and go for the gift she seemed anxious to give him. "If it's a shower massage, we'll plug it right in."

"Not even close," she said, then went to the corner where she'd left the long branch with the shallow fork that she'd picked up on her wood-hauling outing. "It's not a luxury item; it's a necessity. I hope it works. I'll fix some padding over the top of it for your sensitive skin." She held the crutch out to him. "What do you think?"

"I think you've got Florence Nightingale beat all to hell. Get me up, honey. I feel like singin' in the rain."

The rain slanted into their faces and made streamlets over their bodies as Elaina squeezed liquid soap from a plastic container and rubbed it over him vigorously. The lemon scent mixed with the fresh scent of rainwater. To drive the chill away, she kept the fire fixed in her mind. Sky bent to let her wash his hair, and the steady downpour provided a good rinsing. When his turn came, he used one hand to smooth soap over her while he gripped the crutch in the other, holding his left foot at an angle behind him. He washed her hair, too, and her breasts and her belly. It was good to have a cold water dousing, he thought. In a warm, comfortable shower with Elaina the washing would have been cut short.

When they went inside the crackling fire was waiting for them. They shook themselves like puppies, tossing their hair to create little showers of their own. They shivered and shuddered, brushed water from one another with their hands, then let the fire do the rest. Elaina brought their bed closer to the fire, and Sky dropped down on it gratefully, propping his foot on a rock. Elaina took out her medicines and applied antiseptic and fresh bandages where they were needed. Sky's hair dried as it had fallen, in shiny black disarray, but he combed hers, fanning it out before the fire's heat. It was silken from the rainwater, and it gleamed with a soft gold patina in the firelight.

She would do him a service in return, she decided, and she moved behind him to knead the soreness from his back. The sound of his satisfied groan found kindred satisfaction in her. Pleasure given mingled with pleasure received. She knelt behind him, and he tilted his head back into the comfortable nook between her breasts. His hair felt like mink, and it was too luxuriant not to be worn next to her skin. She walked her fingers over his chest, closing in on his flat nipples. When she touched them, he shivered and whispered, "You're a sorceress, Elaina."

"Would you like to be my apprentice?" she suggested, her mouth close to his ear.

"Tell me your secrets."

"Be careful," she warned as he caught his breath. "Once the words are said, they can't be taken back."

"Tell me the words."

"They're powerful, Sky. Maybe too powerful."

With eyes closed he moved his head slowly, side to side against her breasts. She kissed his forehead, and he swallowed hard. "Could you hand me my billfold, Elaina? I think I may need it."

"There's no charge for my magic charm."

"I know. But there are risks associated with mine."

She did as he asked, and because he pleased her beyond fantasy, she did as he asked again and again. His limitations made his gifts seem all the sweeter in comparison, and there were no bounds on his willingness to give. The storm outside was letting up, the rain becoming a gentle trickle. Inside, gentleness became a fierce restraint as the need to become, impossibly, one flesh became torrential.

"I know the words, Elaina."

"They'll bind me if I say them."

"I'll say them, then. I love you."

"Sky..."

"I love you. Oh, Elaina..." He steadied her against the tremors that shook her and gave himself over to his own burst of energy. "Shazam," he growled, and their shared ecstasy shattered into a thousand pieces.

Night fell, and they ate, dozed, lazily explored each other, slept and made love again. The rain had stopped, and they knew they had to leave at daybreak, but any mention of the journey was carefully avoided. This was no longer simply time on their hands. Time was suspended, and they wouldn't think about leaving this mountain womb until the time for leaving came.

They watched the sky lighten, and they held each other, saying little. The world outside brightened, and what had been a gray vista became green and blue in the light of the sun.

"We have to go," he said finally.

"Not yet," she pleaded. "Just a little more time."

"It's been good, hasn't it?"

"It was so scary at first," she remembered with wonder. "And then it became...so special. I think I'd be happy as a cavewoman."

"We could stay."

"Your bones would mend on their own."

"I'd walk with a slight limp, but that would add to my character."

"We'd run out of supplies, but we'd become self-sufficient."

"*I'd* run out of supplies, and I'd end up delivering that baby after all."

They laughed as their eyes projected images on the ceiling to their imaginations' delight. Then he toyed with her hair while other images took over for him. "When I made love to you by the lake, I was at my best, Elaina. I was all in one piece, and my technique was great, don't you think?"

"Um-hmm."

"I didn't like the idea of being awkward. A man in my situation has a certain image to . . . contend with, I guess."

"I didn't even think about—"

"Neither did I," he told her quickly. "I made love to you by the lake, and it was the beginning, but I decided I didn't want to see it through. You made sex more than what it was, more than what it's always been for me, and you scared the hell out of me."

"I thought it was beautiful," she said, and her voice took on a defensive edge.

"I thought so, too. Elaina, I saw you sitting there all by yourself in that bar the other night, and I thought you were beautiful. You danced with me, you let me drive you out to Silver Moon, and I figured I knew where I stood. So I gave it a shot, and you came with me on this jaunt. The interlude by the lake was what I came up here for, that and a little riding and fishing."

Elaina felt a flush of heat in her cheeks, and a wild rush of confusion filled her brain. *Interlude*, her brain repeated. Her limbs stiffened.

"I wasn't looking for what we had up here," he said softly. "I didn't even know it existed. I didn't know you could scare me the way you did when you went out in that storm. I didn't know you could touch me like you did when you . . . whenever you touched me. Hell, Elaina, 'making love' is just what the words imply. Did you know that? I didn't."

"I . . ." She took a steadying breath. "I like to portray it like that."

"Yeah, well, you go right on portraying it that way, and maybe someday the guys of this world will wake up and smell the roses. Or the coconut." He turned his face into her hair, squeezing her shoulders in exuberant delight. The hell with Columbus; Sky Hunter had discovered the New World. His senses ran riot with it. "Or lemon. Lemon's great, too. What's Fast Horse's favorite scent?"

"Lilac water." She made a hollow wish that he would forget about *Swift* Horse.

"Lilacs," he mused. "That could get to me, too. I think you could even wear Mentholatum and I'd like it."

"I think we should start back," she said quietly. She couldn't handle too much more "technique."

"You're right." He sighed when she sat up. "It won't be any joy ride, I guess, but we'll take our time, and we'll get there in good shape."

Sky watched Elaina dress, and he assumed that her silence signaled her regrets. He felt the same way. He managed to get into his own clothes, and he asked her to pack the remains of his left boot. He was dousing the last of the burning coals with dirt when he heard the sound of hoofbeats—a single horse. Rick? John? he wondered. Elaina looked up, too, in time to watch the gray packhorse trot past the cave on his way to greener pastures.

It was several minutes before either of them said anything. The weight of their loss was overwhelming. Without the horse, Sky would have to walk somehow. Without the horse his leg might be damaged beyond repair. Walking away from this situation would take monumental effort. Sky took some time to brace himself.

"He might have run out of grass," he suggested finally, as though the horse had had a reason for deserting them and the reason somehow mattered. "When that happens, they usually find a way to get loose."

"I probably made a mess of the knots. I tried to make them the way you showed me, but everything was wet, and I was in a hurry." The new worry pushed the old ones aside. Sky needed that horse. Elaina couldn't see how he'd make it without a horse, and she'd been careless and lost it.

"We'll have to make some choices," Sky said. "We can't carry all this stuff."

"You can't carry anything."

He looked down at his leg. The swelling had gone down, but once he started walking on it, it would balloon again in no time. He could forget the other boot. How the hell would he make it down this mountain with one bare foot? "We'll just have to take our own sweet time on this trek, Elaina. As long as we can make fire and find shelter, I think we've got enough provisions. We'll make ourselves a couple of backpacks out of one sleeping bag and the tarp."

Elaina needed no further instruction. All he had to do was make it sound possible, and she was convinced that it would be. No need to panic, she told herself. Backpacks. Of course. She'd pack all the food, one aluminum pan, matches, the hunting knife and the whetstone. "What are the bare essentials for fishing?"

Not a complaint out of her, Sky marveled. Not one I-told-you-so. Damn, she was plucky. He grinned, thinking of how hard he'd fallen in the hours since he'd gone over that cliff. "The ol' hook, line and sinker, honey."

They looked as though they were ready to recreate one of Sky's wilderness movies, she thought a little while later. Sky's backpack was lashed around his middle, and Elaina had fashioned rope handles for hers, padding them as best she could. She'd never learned to pack sparingly, and Sky had had to be firm with her about leaving things behind.

They set off at a snail's pace, but once Sky had a little practice on his crutch, he was able to move faster. The wet ground gave him trouble on the slopes, and he often caught his balance with a hand on Elaina's shoulder. He chose a route that would take them away from the steep ledge, and soon they were hobbling through meadows and forests. Despite their slow, careful pace, Sky felt the swelling returning in his ankle.

Elaina didn't ask about distance or the terrain ahead. She took each hill as it came, letting Sky worry about direction. He knew where he was going, and she was going with him. They'd get there eventually. They stopped, ate a little dried fruit or jerked beef, and then moved on. As the rest stops became more frequent, she told herself that "eventually" they could be stretched to fit Sky's needs. They'd take their time; they'd be fine.

Sky knew where he was going, and she was going with him. Another steep grade, more mud, more loose gravel. Beyond this stretch, it would get better, she told herself. They'd find a cold stream and a grove of pines. They'd have more dried beef and a cool drink, and they'd joke about sore feet. Meanwhile, they made progress with each step.

For Sky the first steps had been a challenge. The next mile was hard work, and each succeeding step became an even greater piece of agony. He tried to hold his foot up behind him, but it grew heavier all the time. It felt like half a ton of throbbing flesh and tortured bone. Each time he let the foot touch the ground in an automatic response to his determined effort to walk, white-hot pain shot the length of his leg. Get used to it, he told himself. Mind over matter. But the pain, once a dull ache, had become exquisite.

The swift mountain stream was a thing of beauty. They could see it from the hill, and its promise gave them both a little boost. It got closer by pathetically small degrees, but they kept their eyes straight ahead and saw themselves flopping on its grassy banks. They could not look at one another as they plodded toward the goal they'd silently set. Seeing each other's pain or fear would have destroyed their will to keep moving.

They'd reached the little grove of pines several yards from the stream when Elaina allowed herself a sideways glance. Sky's face was beaded with sweat, his hair plastered to his temples, and his face contorted in a ghastly grimace. Without a word, she dropped her pack and untied his before she all but carried him the rest of the way. He was trembling inside when he lay down in the grass and let his foot dangle in the cold water. The shock of it made him cry out as he closed his eyes against spots of black oblivion. It was a moment before he realized that Elaina had broken the silence. Perhaps more than a moment; she'd had time to fetch their packs.

"Sip it slowly," she was saying. "It's ice cold."

Propping himself on his elbow, he accepted the pan of water and drank from it eagerly. She'd intended to hold the pan for him, but he had enough pride left to do that much himself. It was late afternoon, and they'd made precious little progress.

"We'll stop here for the night," he told her as he handed the water back to her. She'd already started unloading things, but it was important to him to make the actual decision. With a derisive smile he mumbled to his namesake above him, "So says the faithful Indian guide."

"What did you say?"

"Just that we'll camp here tonight." The clouds were high white puffs, and he had a fleeting thought that he should try sending out smoke signals for help. He pictured himself with blanket and fire, working feverishly to form a giant SOS against the blue sky. His smile became genuine as his imagination touched the clouds.

"You found us a good spot. We've come a long way today, haven't we?" she asked encouragingly.

We've got a hell of a long way to go, he thought disparagingly. "Yeah, we're doing pretty well. We'll follow this stream until it plummets through some rough country. Then we'll cut back through the forest. Eventually we'll hit a trail."

Eventually. Eventually sounded promising enough to satisfy Elaina. She rummaged through her supply of dried foods, foil pouches and plastic bags, and wondered aloud, "What should we do about supper?"

"I'm going to haul it out of the water just as soon as you unpack my gear," he promised. The grass felt good under his back, and the water felt good on his leg. He hoped it would take her a good, long time to find his gear.

"Here it is—hook, line and sinker, plus a couple of other doodads. Do you want them now?"

"Sure. You hungry?"

She laughed. "I could eat a whole moose!"

Another image flashed in his mind, and he grinned at the sky again. "If one floats by, I'll be sure and snag him. I'd like to see you eat a whole moose."

Elaina looked at her situation as a series of challenges to her creativity. She left Sky to his fishing and set about gathering wood, hunting for branches and anything that was movable and usable. A pole lashed between two trees served as the frame for a lean-to. She picked through a deadfall and uncovered a rotting log. Hurrying to Sky with it, she cried, "Look what I found!"

Sky flinched when the wood, crawling with grubs, was held under his nose. "What the—"

"Bait," she announced proudly. "Don't you need bait?"

He tipped his head back and howled. "Elaina Delacourte!" he choked out, shaking his head. "Will you look what you've got in your hands?"

"I'm just holding it by the edges," she pointed out. "I'm not touching them. Aren't they great? You could fish for days."

"How times change us," he said, chuckling again. "Put it down here, honey. Just for that, I'm going to catch the fattest trout that ever was spawned and lay it at your feet."

"Cleaned," she reminded him. He'd looked pretty bad when they'd arrived at this spot, but the strain in his face had almost disappeared. She felt cheered by the power of her own initiative. "I thought I'd need your help setting up camp, but I'm managing by myself. Woman's work, you know."

"You call me if you need any muscle," he teased.

She hooked one arm and flexed. "I've got my own."

"Let me feel that." He reached up, but she turned and ran away, laughing.

The lean-to was a masterpiece right out of the pages of her last novel. Pine branches formed the roof, and she'd found enough for a solid thatch. She put the firepit in front, not too close, but close enough so that she could keep a small fire going all night to ward off wildlife. She didn't feel that she could wrestle a bear. Not yet. Dry pine needles made a good mattress under their bed, so she amassed a thick pile under the tarp. In addition to the tarp, they had one sleeping bag, and they had each other.

Sky was amazed. The city dude had become a Boy Scout, or else she'd hired one to make herself look good. The lean-to was straight out of the manual—not that he'd read it himself, but he'd taken some troops out on pack trips. Glowing with pride, Elaina came out from behind the structure, and Sky gave a low whistle. "Give that woman a merit badge," he quipped. He was proud of her, too.

The fattest trout that was ever spawned tasted like ambrosia and answered their bodies' craving for fresh food. After supper Elaina insisted that Sky soak his foot some more, though she knew that when he started walking on it in the morning, it would swell up again. He had begun to place more weight on it as the day passed. She'd seen that, and she'd seen that it was unavoidable. There were two questions she refused to ask: how much farther, and how much more can you stand?

"Do you think ol' Fast Horse and I could have been buddies?" Sky asked as he dangled his feet beside hers in the cold stream. "You think we could have gone out chasing buffalo and wagon trains together?"

"If you could have gotten his name right. It's *Swift* Horse."

"Well, yeah," he agreed with a shrug. "He'd have had to get mine right, too. When you sing your friend's praises, you have to get the guy's name right. They did that, you know. They sang each other's praises. It was important to be recognized for bravery and resourcefulness."

"Swift Horse would have been glad to sing your praises," Elaina assured him. "You bear your pain with the best of men."

"Better to bear it like the best of women. You women know how to survive pain. You keep things going when the men are ready to quit."

"If I'd broken my ankle, you'd be carrying me piggyback down this mountain, and you know it."

"You're damn right I would." He pulled himself up straight and went through the motions, his voice full of conviction. "I'd sling you right up there and shoulder those packs, and I'd march right down this mountain, kicking the bears out of my path. Boy, you'd be…" He cocked an eyebrow at her. "When we come up here next year, you're not gonna test this out, are you?"

"We're coming up here *next* year?"

"I thought we'd make it an annual event." They gazed at one another, eyes full of fun. "I'll sing your praises, Elaina. I'll tell the whole world how brave and resourceful you were up here.'' He jerked his chin toward the round, red, setting sun. "Starting with him.''

The Sioux song he sang in the traditional nasal tones was the only one he knew—a flag song he'd learned in school. The monotonous chant carried across the water and into the trees and made Elaina shiver with awe. The words, even if she'd known them, were indistinguishable, but the tone seemed to echo beyond time. For several moments after his voice plummeted for the final note, she could say nothing.

"What did you sing?" she asked finally.

"I don't remember exactly what the words mean, but in my mind, I was singing about you. I was telling the sun what a hell of a woman I've got here.''

"Really?''

"Really. And it's the first time I've touched base with anything traditional in a long time.''

"It was beautiful. You have a beautiful voice.''

He chuckled and reached over to touch her hair, because he needed to touch base with her, too. "How can you tell?''

"By the way you made my heart pound," she told him quietly.

He wondered if she had any idea what she did to him with those wide-eyed looks of hers. She drew him into her with them, he thought. Then he leaned toward her without thinking, and she raised her chin in anticipation of his kiss.

Chapter Ten

Sky lay with his leg suspended in another of Elaina's slings and his arms folded behind his head. She was asleep beside him. From what he'd seen, she was a morning person. Sky loved nights. Dark and light; Othello and Desdemona. Dramatists would foresee tragedy. He was a Leo, and she was a Scorpio. Well-respected astrologers would predict a clash. He was an "innie" and she was an "outie"; even naval contemplators would take a dim view. He loved comparing notes and finding contrasts, because he thought that made her all the more interesting. He enjoyed defying fate.

He dealt with life through action, while she was an observer, and little got by her. When the time came to act, she knew what she was about. He played his charm for all it was worth, while she sat back and enjoyed its effects, but she was steadfast. When the charm wore thin, she was still there. She let him know how she felt, and she wasn't embarrassed about it. She was soft and warm, but there was nothing fluffy about her. He wanted her in his life.

The breeze rustled the dry branches in the roof that slanted away from his head. It was the kind of shelter he dreamed of when he watched the city at night from the window of his apartment in West Hollywood. There were times when he just wanted clean mountain air and a lean-to, or a wickiup made of curved willows, or even a squaw cooler, with its dry cottonwood branches, like the ones he'd helped his mother build so many summers past. He'd often slept under those simple shelters on summer nights and watched this same bright Western sky.

The night was a black hoop skirt stitched with silver jewels. The fire burned low, tossing up its tiny yellow imitations of stars like so much costume jewelry. Sky knew he'd understated his intentions when he told Elaina he'd come on this trip just for the riding and fishing. This was the kind of night he'd needed to rediscover. He needed those croaking bullfrogs by the stream and the crickets singing from their little pockets in the trunks of the pines. Riding and fishing weren't the half of it. And Elaina had become the essence of the whole picture.

He wasn't sure he'd ever loved anyone before. He'd said the words from time to time because they'd been there to say, and saying them could be quite effective. When he said them to Elaina, they became more than words. They were part of a vision of the rest of his life. Now he was scared, raw edge scared. He didn't want that vision to die up here on this mountain.

How far were they from the Silver Moon trails? Twenty miles, maybe? How many miles had they covered today? Three, maybe four? The trek wasn't going to get any easier. He had to stop more often as the pain ate up his strength. He prayed that it wouldn't touch his will.

He shifted his weight to his right hip. His left ached. If he ever got back to normal, he swore he'd never sleep on his back again. He didn't want Elaina listening to him snore. She would only hear genteel sounds coming from his mouth like, "Buy as many as you want, dear," and "Would you prefer Paris or St. Peter's Island this spring?" If he ever got her out of this mess, he'd give her romance, and he wouldn't do it by tossing her over the rump of some scruffy paint horse. He never could figure out what was meant by the term "noble savage." The words sounded mutually exclusive. He could be noble, all right, and he was determined to show Elaina just *how* noble. Savage? Nibbling her neck was about as savage as he ever wanted to get.

She wiggled closer to him, kissed his shoulder and, without opening her eyes, whispered, "Please get some sleep, love. It'll all work out."

Love. Was she talking in her sleep? He kissed her forehead and closed his eyes. He wanted to believe her—that it would all work out, and that he was her love.

The morning sun poured like warm honey over Elaina's head and shoulders. Beneath her pack her back had begun to sweat, and her underarms were raw from the straps. The padding she'd improvised under the rope needed continual adjustment, and she'd already been sore by the end of the previous day. She longed to be free of encumbrances. After two days of rain, the sunshine gave her the urge to run free through the yellow-green meadow grass.

She saw herself tripping barefoot amid the purple and white wildflowers. In her mind she reached a rocky pinnacle and spun around, breaking into song. Able to make do with what nature provided, she had met the mountains, and they were hers. She could have been Daniel Boone or Johnny Appleseed. She'd provided fire and shelter, she'd cooked, and she was certain she could learn to provide food, too. Surely she was no longer a dude. She'd conquered the wilderness.

Sky was battling on another front, though he moved along a path parallel to hers. He, too, suffered from a sore armpit and a constricting encumbrance. He'd also begun suffering momentary blackouts from the pain. So far he'd been able to walk through most of them. At other times he had suggested a short rest, hoping Elaina wouldn't notice the extent of his plight. He had to get her as close to the trails as he could. Then what? He couldn't think that far ahead. Just get as close to the trails as possible, he told himself as he tried to make a maze of vague black spots disappear.

"Oh, look, Sky!" Elaina whispered. He stopped and tried to focus, but she walked ahead, stalking. "They don't see us. We must be upwind or something."

A bull moose and two cows. Sky straightened as his head cleared. "Where in hell did he come . . . Elaina, get back here." The last part was a guttural whisper, and while Elaina didn't respond, the moose did. Three huge heads turned in Elaina's direction. The cows were homely creatures, but the bull's stately rack, its curves and hollows defined in the morning sun, gave him a regal dignity.

"Isn't he magnificent?" she whispered, creeping closer. "Look at those horns."

"Elaina, stand still," Sky pleaded.

The bull lowered his head and stood his ground. Elaina stood hers. A cold rush of fear propelled Sky forward, and he put his weight on the injured leg without even thinking. "Just back away slowly," he murmured as he moved in front of her. The moose snorted at the ground, while his cows retreated into the trees. "Do as I say," Sky ordered brusquely.

Elaina hesitated, then moved back slowly. "Would he...?"

"Be ready to run, but don't make any sudden moves yet." Sky readied the only weapon he had—the crutch that had taken him this far down the mountain. The moose raised his head, displaying the broad sweeping shovels of his antlers. In a bold gesture Sky brandished his crutch and hissed. The moose seemed to study the man for a moment. Then he swung his head in the direction his cows had taken and trotted after them.

Elaina moved to Sky's side, putting her shoulder under his arm. The strength seemed to drain from his body, and he dropped his chin to his chest, shaking his head.

"Sky, you're standing on your—you *walked* on it. Sky, you might have..."

"*You* might have been killed." His voice rose as his fear gave way to anger. "That was no little deer; that was a bull moose with his cows. They'll charge when they think they're cornered."

"Can you walk? I don't know which way we should go, Sky, but you can't just—"

"*You* can't *just*! This isn't one of your books, Elaina. This is real; these animals are wild. You can't just walk up to a bull moose out here, for God's sake!"

"Sky," she said quietly, "sit down. Please."

He scanned the area. Beyond the meadow there were junipers and ponderosa pines, a cutbank and a ravine. If he sat down right here, in the middle of the field, he knew he wouldn't get up. "We'll rest over there," he told her, pointing to a stand of pines. Leaning heavily on Elaina, with his crutch under his left arm, he made it across the meadow. Elaina unloaded their packs.

Sky slid to the ground, propping his back against a fallen log. Tilting his head back, he took several deep breaths and turned to Elaina. "If he'd been in rut, he probably would have charged."

"Doesn't rutting season come in the fall?" She sat cross-legged next to him and studied his face. The strain in his jaw told her that his teeth were clamped tight and that he was in terrible pain.

"Yes, it comes in the fall, and I've known several hunters who've been treed by moose."

"So in the summer they're not as—"

"They're wild animals all year long." He lifted his head and delivered a level stare. "You know what they see in the summer? Idiot tourists who think they're at a zoo. People who think they can walk right up for a nice close-in shot with their cameras."

"I didn't have a camera." She glanced away. "I'm sorry, Sky. I wasn't thinking. I didn't even realize I was moving toward them. They were just so beautiful."

She heard his long, hollow sigh, and it was a moment before she allowed herself to look him in the face again. When she did, she found that he was resting his eyes and working the muscles in his jaw. "How could your ankle bear your weight like that?'' she asked finally. He didn't answer. ''I made it worse, didn't I?''

''*I* did what I did,'' he said quietly. ''I wasn't thinking, either.''

''Do you think we could bind it somehow, or splint it?'' He winced as she carefully lifted his ankle into her lap and peeled his sock away. The swelling stretched the purple and green bruises into large splashes of sickening color and distorted the shape of his leg to such an extent that it was hard to tell whether the grotesque angles were formed by swollen tissue or shattered bone.

Elaina's stomach tightened in sympathetic pain as she bent to kiss a terrible bruise. ''How were you able to come between that moose and me?'' she asked, looking up into his face. ''If he had charged, you wouldn't have been able to run.''

He had no idea how his ankle had supported him, though he knew he'd run several feet on it. All he'd seen was that great rack and this small woman threatened, attacked, injured. ''He could have tossed you up in the air like a scarecrow.''

''And you.''

He closed his eyes and shook his head. ''You've got to be more cautious, Elaina. I can't protect you.''

''But you did, Sky, without a thought for yourself. No thought for images or how a man's supposed to act. You weren't *acting* at all. That wasn't masculine pride; that was human courage.''

He didn't have the strength to be embarrassed. She'd just kissed his foot, and he couldn't even be embarrassed about that. He figured pain must take all the starch out of a man. He'd have to go for another belt in karate or something when he got back to civilization. What was he on—brown? He wondered if the moose would have been impressed.

"What are you smiling about?"

He opened his eyes, and her beauty struck him. Her nose was sunburned, her hair was tied back at the base of her neck, and her eyes were gray and watery. "You." It was a thin smile, but it was the best he could do. "You and your moose. Aren't you the one who was sure a bear was bound to attack her in her tent a few days ago?"

"Bears have claws and big teeth. Everybody knows bears are dangerous."

He motioned for her to come closer and sit beside him. She propped his leg on the bedroll, noting that each movement caused him difficulty. Then she settled next to him, rested her back against the log and avoided any real discussion of her fears.

"A bull moose weighs over half a ton and has huge antlers," Sky told her. "A buffalo has smaller horns and a meaner disposition. Cougars have the teeth and claws you seem to have sense enough to respect, and they have the added advantage of being able to pounce on you from above. And then there are badgers, coyotes, even porcupines—"

"Oh, come on, Sky, they're not going to attack me if I don't bother them."

"A moose might consider your walking up to introduce yourself to be a bother."

"Okay." She held a hand up in surrender. "I'll behave myself from now on. Very careful, very cautious—I won't make a move without your advice."

"And with my advice?" He pressed his palm to hers, and they laced their fingers together. "Will you follow my instructions until we get back, Elaina?"

"I've *meant* to all along."

"I like to think I'm still the guide here." He winked at her. "Humor me."

She smiled. "Advise me, then."

He hooked his arm around her shoulders as he lowered their clasped hands to his lap. The pain in his ankle was killing him, but he savored the feeling that she needed him. "You could use some of that first-aid cream on your nose. It's going to peel."

"Then it'll match the rest of me." Their hands made an interesting study linked together like that, she thought. Large fingers laced with small. She liked the contrast of the dusky brown against the delicate cream. It made her feel feminine despite her chipped nails and scraped skin.

"You did get a little sunburned up there at the lake, didn't you?"

"You noticed." She'd wondered why he hadn't mentioned the fact that she was a pretty shade of pink everywhere.

"Noticed? Honey, I took great pleasure in watching you sizzle." She looked surprised, and he gave her a squeeze and laughed. "Pardon me, I stood *watch* over you," he corrected. "Must be the Fast Horse in me."

"*Swift* Horse. Why didn't you . . ." They both realized what was on the tip of her tongue, and they laughed together. So she'd wanted him to catch her. So he'd stubbornly resisted. They could laugh now that they weren't playing those roles anymore. "Next time, let me know you're there."

"If you'll let me know I'm welcome."

"Truthfully," she admitted with a shrug, "I was waiting for you. That's why I got a little overdone."

"I'll put the first-aid cream wherever you need it," he promised, "if you'll do something for me."

"Of course. What?"

The laughter was gone, and his eyes were filled with pain again. "Go down to Silver Moon. Get me some help."

She dropped her head on his shoulder and hugged him close. "I wish I could."

"You could build me one of your little Boy Scout houses, leave me some firewood, and I could tell you how to—"

"No!" She drew back, terrified that he might be serious. "No, Sky. I'd lose my way. One mountain looks like another to me, one tree like all the rest. Pretty soon I wouldn't be able to find you, either, and I'd be totally lost."

"You'd blaze a trail."

"No. I'm staying with you."

"Elaina..."

"I'm staying with you, Sky. I'd be lost otherwise."

It was advice he hadn't really wanted her to take, but he didn't know what else to suggest. She was right; self-sufficient as she'd become, she had no sense of direction that he could discern. She needed street signs, and he'd led her even beyond the range of trail markers. It was up to him to get her out of this mess— *personally.*

"I've been thinking, Elaina. How about some kind of splint?"

She nodded, offering a brave smile. "What . . . how would we do that?"

"Let's experiment. Everything else you've tried has worked." He frowned, considering. "In your book, Fast Horse's woman tears up her petticoat for bandages. You don't have a petticoat, do you?" He raised his brow at her negative gesture. "Guess you'll just have to tear your shirt into strips. Maybe your jeans, too."

"I've got a better idea," she offered, reaching for his top button. "How about *your* shirt and *your* jeans? All this ripping up of clothes tends to get a little one-sided."

It wasn't easy to tease anymore. She made a feeble grab for his shirt, and he fended her off halfheartedly. But she took comfort in the fact that he was smiling, and they were still together. It was the bedroll she decided to sacrifice. She tore yards of bandaging and used the stuffing for padding. With stout sticks and painstaking wrapping, she fashioned a kind of cast below his knee. The swelling disturbed her, and she wasn't sure this was the right thing to do. She was certain that the worst thing for him to do was to walk on it.

They made little progress. Even without his pack, Sky's burden had become too great. The arm Elaina braced around him was wet with the sweat from his back, and she felt him struggle to control his trembling each time he inched his weight forward.

"We're stopping for lunch, Sky. I see a good place to prop up your foot."

"Any place that isn't spinning would be fine."

The ground felt wonderful. Anything that didn't require him to walk was welcome. Sky watched the tops of the trees dance circles above his head as he wiped his brow on his sleeve. If only she could just roll him down the hills, he thought. He could wait for her at the bottom, and then she could roll him down the next one. God, he was going crazy.

"Here, drink some of this."

This time he let her hold the container to his mouth, and he took a long pull. He nearly choked. "That's pretty potent water," he sputtered.

"You're having a two-martini lunch today, Mr. Hunter."

"There wasn't that much left in the bottle," he remembered, screwing up his face against the fiery taste.

"Let's pretend there was. Let's pretend you don't have to worry about getting back to work. Just relax."

He turned his head away from the offer of a second sip and muttered, "Get me something to eat. I'm already seeing double."

She handed him a piece of beef jerky. "There isn't anything else to drink," she told him. "I'm afraid you'll dehydrate."

"We aren't far from water."

"Are you sure?"

He eyed her as steadily as he could manage. She thought he'd lost his bearings, he realized. She figured he was totally out of it, that he'd gotten them lost. He might have caused them a lot of problems, but being lost wasn't one of them. "I know where we are," he assured her. "But if I drink that stuff, I won't. Put it away. *Throw* it away."

"But the pain is too..."

One shot of Everclear had actually cleared his head, and he didn't like what he saw. His stalwart hiking partner was wild-eyed with fear. "Too what, honey?"

"You hurt so bad, Sky. Every step..." She closed her eyes and laid her head against his chest. "I just hate it."

He put his arms around her and ran one hand up and down her back, hoping she wasn't crying. His love for her squeezed harder at his insides than any physical pain. "There was a time in my life," he told her in a quiet, steady voice, "when I would have given any painkiller a try. I would have taken any fear-quencher, any courage-stimulator. Right now, if I thought I could drink that stuff and be able to get you out of this mess, I'd drain the bottle. I'd do anything, take anything, to avoid hurting you like this." He held her quietly for a moment, feeling her heart beat against his chest. "I think you've about reached the same point, haven't you?"

She managed a strangled "Yes," and he lifted her away from him and made her look at him. "I just wanted you to stop hurting for a little while."

"Then don't lose your faith in me." He gave her a wistful smile, his eyes full of dark sadness. "My faith in you has grown by leaps and bounds, while yours..." He shook his head slowly. "Don't tell me I'd be just as good to you drunk as I am sober. I'd hate to think you believed that."

"What I believe is that I did something very stupid and caused you more pain," she told him. If she talked quickly, she wouldn't cry, she thought, and she fought the panic, struggled against the burning in her throat. The last thing she wanted to do was sit here and bawl. "We wouldn't have to push so hard, except for your injury. If it's badly broken and we don't get help soon, the damage might be...they might not be able to repair it completely. But if we do push hard and you get worse—sick or some kind of infection—either way..."

He laid a finger over her lips, then smoothed her hair with the same hand. "Surely you remember what one of our chiefs said once. 'The people are not defeated until the hearts of their women are on the ground.' "

The words caught her fancy, and she pursed her lips as she turned them over in her mind. "No, I...I don't remember."

"Then your repertoire of Indian wisdom was incomplete. Our women are tenacious, and when we see them giving up, we know we're lost." His hand came to rest on her shoulder, and he squeezed it gently until she looked into his eyes. "Is my woman's heart on the ground?" he asked gently.

Though it was only rhetorical, a phrase made to echo a quotation, she took the words "my woman" and hugged them to her heart as she smiled and whispered, "No."

"I know where we are, honey. I know which way we have to go. Believe me, I haven't gotten us lost."

She was blinking hard against the threat of tears as she pulled herself up and sat on her heels, still bending close to him. "I know. It's just that . . . when you ran in front of me back there, I know something else happened. There was more damage done. There had to be."

"Maybe there was. We'll never know how much damage I did to begin with, and how much I acquired along the way."

"How much damage *you* did! Sky, it was my horse that shied. You got me away from there in time. You took the fall I should have taken. It takes me twice as long to react at a time like that; I don't think!" She thumped her thigh with her fist, but he grabbed her hand before she could repeat the motion.

"I react in a crisis," he admitted, "but you come up with the greatest ideas when you have time to do a little thinking. Your ingenuity has gotten us this far, Elaina."

"But my *carelessness*..."

"Has given me a couple of chances to play the hero. Thank God. A man in my position has a certain—"

"Image to live up to, I know." After a couple of quick swipes at her cheeks, she managed to smile. "How did we do on this splint? Is it too tight? I could probably figure out a way to loosen it up, maybe add some support."

"I was thinking maybe you could improvise some sort of transportation," he teased. "A simple wheelbarrow, or maybe a primitive forklift."

Okay, she would allow herself to laugh, she decided. For his sake, she'd laugh at his jokes while she gathered a few branches and lashed some shelter together. All they had now was the tarp, which, along with the rope and food, she'd considered essential. There were several sturdy branches lying right there for the taking, in fact, and there was ... rope, tarp, poles. "I don't know about a wheelbarrow," she began slowly, her mind putting the pieces together, "but how about a travois?"

"A travois? You need a horse for that."

"You've got me."

He eyed her suspiciously. Damn, she was serious. She actually believed she could pull him in a litter. "No, I don't, Elaina. You break your back, and then where are we?" She was already measuring a pine pole against his height. "It won't work, I'm telling you, and I won't even consider—"

"Just on the downhill slopes, Sky. I know I can't budge you up a hill, but in some places, gravity will give you a boost."

"Elaina . . ."

"Come on, Sky. Let's try."

He helped her with the frame by carving notches in the poles to hold the cross pieces, and then by lashing the contraption together with efficient knots. They came up with a long, narrow triangle strung with a network of rope, which was covered by the tarp to provide a sturdy sling. There was a foot rest, and handles with which to brace himself. He padded the handles she would hold on to to drag the litter, and he beat down the image of her standing in a wooden harness of his making and straining her back against his weight.

It was a good piece of work, they decided together. Sky hobbled to a spot that looked like a promising place to try it out. They were headed downhill, and the sound of running water in the distance was a sufficient lure for Elaina, since she was thirsty. Once she got moving, the going wasn't too bad. She had to wend her way among the pine trees, but their dry, fallen needles made a slick surface for her path. By the time she reached the stream, her arms felt two inches longer, and she needed that drink.

"It's faster this way, don't you think?"

"Yeah." He was feeling a little morose. Not that it wasn't *easier* this way, but he didn't like the idea of her pulling him. He didn't even think he liked the idea that she was *able* to pull him.

"Will we follow this stream for a while?"

"Yeah."

"Is it mostly downhill through these woods?"

"Yeah, pretty much."

"Good. I think the pine needles help."

He sat there looking hard into the trees across the stream.

"Does it still hurt a lot, Sky?" she asked anxiously. "How do you feel?"

"Guilty as hell."

She laid a hand on his shoulder. "It's not that hard, really. It's better than having you lean on me after the pain gets so bad you can hardly move." He glanced at her, one eyebrow arched. "Really, it is. We'll make camp when I get tired, and you'll catch us some fish."

"Most of our camping equipment is tied up in that thing."

"There's some rope left, and we can take the tarp off the travois to cover our bed. I've seen how handy you are with that knife. You can notch the cross-pieces for the lean-to, and we won't need as much rope."

He studied his hands. His fingers were black with pine pitch. "You'll sleep," he told her. "I'll keep the fire going through the night. Without that sleeping bag..."

"We'll get by. We have so far, and the challenges just keep coming. You know what?" She looked at him steadily, her tone serious. "I think this is a very...*interesting* experience."

He caught the look she gave him, and both of them burst into laughter at the same time. "Interesting experience! You are incredible, lady." He lay back on the pine needles and let the laughter take him. The sight of her smiling face was a balm, as well. "When we come back up here next year, you know what I'm gonna do?"

"What?"

"I'm gonna get you a bull moose."

"Oh, no, you wouldn't shoot..."

"Hell, no, I'm gonna catch one. Rope him. Wait'll you see the size loop I can throw. You'll have yourself a pet moose. You can hitch him up to a sleigh or something."

It occurred to her that after this experience she wouldn't ask any animal to pull her around in anything, but she couldn't tell Sky that. "I think my landlady might object."

"There won't be any landlady telling us what to do with our backyard. We're not going to live in an apartment, honey. I'm sick of apartments." He rolled his head to the side so he could see her. "I'll build you whatever kind of a house you want. With a big red moose barn in back."

It was as much a fairy tale as any of her stories, she told herself. It was "interlude" talk. His vulnerable position was temporary. It was just a matter of time before he'd be back in Hollywood, surrounded by bright lights and beautiful people, and then he'd be hard-pressed to remember her name.

But if he could talk a good game for optimism's sake, so could she. "If I could just get a guided tour up here every summer so I could see him in the wild..."

"Whatever you say. I'll put a tag on him and let him go, but everyone will know he's your moose."

She smiled and fluttered her eyelashes. "And everyone will know you're my hero."

"Damn right."

Damn right, she thought, which made her feel like the classic fool, but that would be her secret.

They started down the hill again, and Elaina vowed to walk a mile. She wasn't sure how long a mile was, but the goal kept her going. Her hands chafed, then became sore, and soon they were raw. Sky called for a rest, but she assured him that she wasn't tired and walked on. When she did rest, she hid her hands from him. He massaged her shoulders, then took up his crutch and hobbled for a while before succumbing to the pain. It was true; they made better time with him in the travois. Better time was only relative, though, and their progress was excruciatingly slow.

Elaina wasn't sure what sound she was hearing. Something else was moving through the woods. She stopped and listened.

"Someone's coming," Sky said quietly.

"Or some*thing*."

"No, it sounds like horses." He listened again. "Elaina, it sounds like horses!" He shoved his fingers in his mouth and gave a shrill whistle. "Over here!"

Sky was right. They were horses. Breaking a trail where there was none, three horsemen, one well ahead of the others, came toward them through the trees. "Here they are, Dad. They're... I think they're all right, except..." The last horse passed the other two, and the big man who rode him stood in his stirrups, eyes narrowing under the brim of his hat as he approached the stream.

Joe Two Moon pulled his horse to a stop and stared at the pair before him. "Danny? Is that you or your corpse?"

"I'm not dead, Uncle Joe. I just broke my—"

"Not dead!" Joe roared, dropping to the ground with an agility that belied his bulk. "You've got this woman pulling your worthless carcass down the mountain, and you're not dead? We'll see about that!"

Elaina lowered her burden to the ground, but not soon enough to head off the bear of a man who was thrusting burly arms down toward Sky. "Mr. Two Moon, this was the only way..." She reached out in protest, but then she stepped back to watch the two men hug each other.

With another step backward Elaina removed herself from the reunion. The team she and Sky had become ceased to exist. Someone named Danny had been rescued.

Chapter Eleven

Rick rode back to Silver Moon and telephoned instructions to the air ambulance service in Billings. Joe had chosen a pick-up point that would be accessible to the helicopter and easily visible from the air. It wasn't far, and Sky was given a choice of conveyance—horse or travois. He chose the horse. His pride wasn't served by the awkward way he had to haul himself into the saddle, but at least he was sitting up. Elaina left her travois and her carefully hoarded supplies behind and mounted the other horse that Joe had brought in the hope of finding them safe and able to make the ride home. Taking a seat in the saddle was a relief to her, too.

"It was the horses that tipped us off," Joe explained as he led the way along the bank of the rippling stream. "We found the saddle horses grazing just a few miles above the lodge, and we set out looking. When the pack horse came back, we figured we were on the right track. Did you get up to the lake?"

"Yeah, we did." Sky cherished the details of his trip and had no intention of sharing most of them. In fact, he had no intention of sharing much beyond the facts of his accident. His ankle throbbed, his leg hung limply from the saddle, and he didn't feel like talking at all.

"Catch anything?" Joe persisted.

"Trout."

"You're gonna catch hell from your Aunt Jenny when you see her. You know that, don't you?"

"The helicopter's taking me up to Billings, isn't it?"

"Unless she's told him to stop off at Silver Moon first so she can give you a piece of her mind."

The idea was absurd, but Sky knew it was all that Joe was able to say. He and Jenny had probably spent some words on him first, and then some worry. "Tell her you gave it to me for her."

"You'll have to tell her yourself," Joe said. "She'll be waiting to fuss over Miss Delacourte, and no doubt she'll be up to Billings soon to fuss over you."

"Elaina's going to Billings with me. She needs—she may need medical attention, too." He thought for a minute. "When I do see Aunt Jenny, I've got something to tell her, though. This isn't a man's world up here, the way you always said. She oughta get you to show it to her." Joe's expression became pained, and Sky laughed. "After you get those damned nags of yours used to the hazards of the twentieth century."

The waiting seemed interminable, but at last their alert ears were rewarded by the sound of a distant revolving flutter. They shaded their eyes to watch a gray spot in the sky become a helicopter, which hovered above them for a few moments before dropping into the meadow like a remote control toy at their beck and call.

Though the paramedic had expected only one passenger, he accepted two. Elaina insisted she was fine, but that Sky had taken a bad fall and needed attention. The young man carefully unwrapped Sky's leg and gave it a cursory examination, then assured him dryly that it didn't look good. Sky said he knew that. With a cold stare, he said it didn't feel good, either.

"Let me see those hands, ma'am," the paramedic offered, dismissing Sky's sarcasm and raising his voice in competition with the helicopter's whirring blades. "Looks like you've got some bad rope burns."

"No," Elaina said firmly. "Sky has some rope burns, but I think they're pretty well healed." She held her hands closed. "I just got a little—"

Sky rolled over on his side and reached for her hands. She resisted, but he persisted, and finally she relented. After he studied them, he kissed first one palm, then the other. She felt nothing but the warmth of his breath and the tingling he always sparked when he touched her.

Elaina had been examined, disinfected, bandaged and sent on her way. The doctor heard her story and expressed his admiration. She hadn't torn any muscles, wrenched any shoulders, or dislocated anything in her back, which he considered to be remarkable considering the load she'd carried. He decried the use of light planes to "buzz" anything, saying that he had a pilot's license himself, and he despised those who gave flying a bad name with their pranks. Each time Elaina asked about Sky, she was told that he was with his doctor or in X-ray or resting.

She finally gave up and checked herself into a nearby motel. The bed looked like a small piece of heaven, and she slept for sixteen hours straight. When she called the hospital she was told that Sky was being prepared for surgery. She would have to wait.

Her next problem was money. She'd carried her personal belongings, including her wallet, in the saddle bags that had taken off with her saddle horse. She put through a call to her bank in Minneapolis and arranged to have a line of credit with a Billings bank.

Next she needed something decent to wear. She found a department store and bought two changes of clothes. It felt good to wear a skirt again, but she vowed to give the shirt and the pair of jeans she'd worn through her mountain adventure a place of honor in her closet. Having bolstered her confidence with rest and a new pair of shoes, Elaina went back to the hospital and insisted on seeing Sky. Mr. Hunter was still in surgery, she was told, and it was impossible to predict when he might be back in his room.

Elaina decided to have lunch in the hospital cafeteria, but all she tasted was the coffee. What could be taking so long? He only had a broken ankle. She was no doctor, of course, but she'd invested so much time and anxiety in that ankle that she felt as though she were part owner. On her next trip to the surgical floor she was told that Mr. Hunter was now in recovery. Yes, she would wait, she insisted, and she was directed to his room.

He was conscious but groggy when they wheeled him past her. Elaina watched four attendants help him move from the stretcher to the bed, and she remembered how it had taken only one of her to move him down the mountain. Two nurses fussed over him for several minutes before one finally told him, "You have a visitor, Mr. Hunter. Are you up to—"

"Elaina?"

"I'm here, Sky," she said anxiously, hopping off the chair and moving quickly to the bedside.

"They told me you'd left."

He looked tired. His face seemed thin, and there were shadows under his eyes. "They told me you were indisposed," she said as the nurses backed away and she took her place by his side.

"Five minutes," one nurse said.

"She's staying more than five lousy minutes," Sky insisted, glaring in the direction from which the voice had come. "You let family members stay. Elaina's my...anything you want to name. Part of my family."

"Mr. Hunter..."

"She stays. And whenever she comes to see me, I don't care what time it is, you let her in. Then I'll behave myself and take my medicine."

The nurse gave an affected laugh. "Whatever you say, Mr. Hunter. We want you to be comfortable."

When the woman had gone, Elaina sat on the side of the bed and touched Sky's chest, his shoulder, his cheek, making sure he was there. "How are you? You seem to have endeared yourself to the nurses already."

"I told them I was an actor. They think I know all the stars. How are you?"

"Fine."

"Your hands?" He felt for them.

"They're fine."

"Your arms? Your back? Did I break your back?"

"Fine...fine...no. Sky! You're the one who had surgery, which took forever." She'd seen the cast before they'd covered it with the sheet, and she glanced at the bulge it made at the foot of the bed. "What did they do?"

"My ankle was shattered," he said lightly. "They say it'll take several operations, but I'll be able to— Your sunburn. How's your sunburn?"

"It's fine, Sky. You'll be able to what?"

"I'll be able to get around eventually," he said, smiling as if she were the one in need of consolation. "I probably won't even limp, but if I do—" He shrugged as he watched his fingertip trace a narrow white stripe in her skirt. "Hell, there are plenty of actors with physical handicaps, but not one is an Indian. I'll be unique."

"Sky..."

His fingertip had reached the place where her hands lay folded in her lap, and he raised it like a feeler, testing the back of her hand as he gave words to the anxiety that had distracted him from worrying about mere physical problems. "I thought you'd left."

"No, of course not."

Satisfied, he took her hands in his and gave them a grateful squeeze. She winced. "I'm sorry," he told her quickly and kissed her fingertips. "God, I'm glad you're here."

"I'm glad *you're* here. I was afraid we might not be able to..."

"No, you weren't," he whispered, his eyes losing their focus. "You were never afraid. Damn it, Elaina, they gave me some kind of drug."

"For the pain."

He chuckled. "What pain? Surgery's as easy as falling off a cliff. I wanna go back and get that travois. I wanna mount it on my living room wall."

"Joe will do that for you," she assured him. "I called him, and he's been checking every couple of hours. When you're ready for visitors, he'll be here."

Sky groaned. "Along with Aunt Jenny, my mother, and whatever brothers and sisters they can round up. If I had died, even more of them would have turned out. Indians put on great funerals. Plenty of frybread and potato salad, lots of wailing."

"Shall I bring some potato salad in when the visitors start coming? There's a delicatessen down the street." She touched his chin, which was free of the few bristles he'd sprouted since they'd been together. Elaina wondered which nurse had performed that service for him. "I don't want to worry you, but I think you could do a convincing death scene with no help from makeup."

He was fighting against the heaviness he felt throughout his body as he tried to smile. "Could you manage a little wailing in the background?"

"Sure." She perked up at the thought, her eyes dancing. "I did some wailing in a story once. 'Like the lonesome call of a wolf, deserted by his kind.'"

"I said wailing, not howling. It's gotta be done right; it's for my family." He closed his eyes, and his voice came softly. "Thanks for calling Joe."

"Joe said he'd wait until you felt like seeing people before he came. He also said he called O'Malley." He opened his eyes at the news, and she tilted her head in a curious manner. "Apparently you asked him to."

"Yeah. An agent's worse than a mother. You have to touch base." He smiled and lifted his hand to touch her cheek. Words felt sloshy in his mouth, but he wanted to talk. He wanted an excuse to say her name. "I don't want to see any of them as long as you're here. Stay with me, Elaina."

"I will."

"Even if I . . . I feel kind of drunk, Elaina."

"I know. It's okay. It's legal." She stroked his hair back from his forehead, and he closed his eyes again. "Why did Joc call you Danny?" Elaina wondered.

"That's my name, honey. Dan Sky Hunter. That's who I really . . . am. Elaina," he whispered. "'Laina, Elaina, Elaine. I could make a song . . . out of your name."

"Dan Sky Hunter," she said before she kissed his forehead. "I could make a vow with yours."

"How about poker? I *know* I can beat you at poker. Rummy's for girls."

Elaina tapped the deck of cards against the top of the nightstand and offered a smile. "I beat you at black jack, too."

"Yeah, but you wouldn't bet anything. I play better when there's something at stake. Same with poker." His arched eyebrow gave him a wicked look. "What do you say we make this interesting, Elaina?"

"You mean you want to bet clothes?" she said, cutting the cards and then shuffling them expertly. "Men always want to bet clothes."

"How much would you say you've got to lose?"

"If your nurse came in here and found me naked? Probably all my hair and both eyeballs."

Sky grinned. "She does kinda like me, doesn't she? But seriously—" he set his face for seriousness "—how many pieces of clothing would you say you have on? You can count each shoe separately." Elaina ran through a mental list, keeping track on her fingers. He sighed. "I'd get more of a thrill out of this if you went through that aloud."

"Seven," she announced primly.

He looked wounded. "Have a heart. Look at this— foot up in the air, immobilized. If I ever walk again, it'll probably be with one foot up in the air, and they say I'll be here for weeks. I need a little risqué entertainment, Elaina."

"Seven," she repeated firmly, eyeing the metal frame from which his foot was suspended.

"Okay, seven. Surprise me with what they are. Now—" He motioned for her to deal. Instead she let him cut the cards. "Your odds are good, Elaina. I've only got two pieces of clothing, unless you've got a saw for the cast. All you have to do—" he handed her the cards "—is win the first two hands. Then I'm done for."

"And if I don't?"

"Well, we'll count that necklace, that ring." She glanced at the blue sapphire on her right hand, then touched the little gold heart she wore on a thin gold chain. "What I'm really after is the necklace," he confided. "I'm not looking to win any lacy under-things. Honest."

"Honest Injun?" she teased.

"You're looking at one." He tossed her a wink. "How 'bout it, pilgrim?"

"Dealer's choice?"

"Of course."

She buried the top card and dealt. "Mr. Hunter, the name of the game is five card stud. Jacks or better to open, and the only thing wild is the dealer."

Elaina dealt herself three kings on the first hand. Sky raised an eyebrow and untied his sash. He made a production of slipping his arms out of his robe while Elaina watched, shaking her head at his silliness. She decided it was his business if he wanted to sit there in his hospital gown while he dealt her a hand and called the same game.

Elaina won the second hand with a pair of tens. Laughing, Sky reached for the tie at the back of his neck.

"Don't be ridiculous," she said, feeling comfortably smug as she fanned the cards out on the tray table.

"A bet's a bet." The top strings on his gown came apart. He reached down for the next ones.

"Sky!" Elaina pushed the tray aside and dove for his neck, moving to secure the gown with both hands. "You're crazy. You'd love to have that nurse walk in here and find—"

"Is my patient trying to escape?"

Sprawled across Sky's bed with her arms draped around his neck, Elaina turned a reddening face toward the door. She didn't have the presence of mind to pull away before Sky put his arms around her, and then it was too late.

He was all innocence. "Elaina's expressing her gratitude again, Miss March. I keep telling her it was all in a day's work—you know—saving her life like I did—but she can't seem to leave it at that."

"Saving *my*—"

"It's all right, honey. One more kiss is really all I can handle right now." He moved to plant one on the mouth he'd rendered nearly speechless, and then he let her go. "Behave yourself, now."

Elaina slunk back to her chair, muttering, while Sky charmed the attractive, brown-eyed Miss March with, "If you'd ever been rescued from a cliff, a bolt of lightning and a moose, Miss March, you'd know the true meaning of gratitude. Right now Elaina's feelings are a little out of control."

Sky tilted his head forward while Nurse March retied his hospital gown. "I see what you mean." She produced a pressure cuff from her pocket. "I came to check your vital signs."

"Your timing is perfect then." He offered his arm. "If I'm high, bring me an ice pack."

"If you're high, we might have to supervise Elaina's visits," Miss March suggested with a hint of a smile as she stuck a thermometer in his mouth.

He glanced at Elaina and grinned, rolling the thermometer under his tongue. "That probably won't be necessary. I doubt if I'll get any gratitude out of her for a while now. You mad at me, honey?" he asked.

"Why should I be? The fact of the matter is, Miss March, that I beat the man at his own game."

"Ohhh, they hate that." As she made some notes on her chart, the nurse asked, "What was it?"

"Strip poker," Elaina said flatly, and she raised a coy eyebrow in Sky's direction. "Stud."

The nurse gathered her instruments. "I'll bring the ice pack and a chess board."

As soon as Miss March was gone, Sky flashed an evil grin. "Wanna play strip chess?"

"You can't take your clothes off in the presence of queens and bishops."

"Ah, but those knights   "

"You just want to pawn my jewelry."

Sky surrendered, but he went down laughing. "Okay, okay, so you choose the game. What's it gonna be, Elaina?" He picked up the deck of cards and fanned through it with his thumb. "Old maid?"

"Now there's a stereotype if I've ever heard one."

His smile disappeared. "You're right, it is. We're stuck in a lot of them, aren't we?"

"A woman can choose not to be married," she continued. "If she isn't married, it doesn't mean it wasn't her choice, and it doesn't mean she's going to shrivel up into a cranky old crone."

"No, it doesn't. But if a woman *wants* to accept a man as part of her life, there's nothing wrong with—"

A voice outside the door interrupted the progress they might have made. "Sky Hunter, you're going to be the death of me yet!" O'Malley breezed in looking California cool in his white slacks and royal blue polo shirt. He didn't wait for an invitation before pulling up a chair beside Sky's bed. "Hello, Miss Delacourte. How's our boy?"

"Hello, Mr. O'Malley," Elaina returned. "You'll have to ask him."

"Sky, I make it my business to look after your interests. The least you can do is look after your body. What's this about a broken ankle?"

"What you see is what you get, O'Malley."

O'Malley surveyed the bed, the sling, the cast and the crutches in the corner. "I'll take it, and so will Pinnacle. I explained the situation to them as I pieced it together from your uncle and your doctor—"

"Why didn't you talk to me?"

"We haven't been communicating too well lately." O'Malley smiled indulgently. The boy had suffered an attack of artistic conscience and gone through the predictable soul-searching routine. Now he was in love, a state of mind that would bring about another predictable set of changes in his behavior. Amateur psychologist that he was, O'Malley knew the score, and he was more optimistic about dealing with the temporary insanity of love than with the serious problem of actor-turned-artist.

"Pinnacle understands your situation, and they think there may be a fit for you in a high-budget production somewhere down the road. Right now—" he grinned, and a dollar sign appeared to flash in each of his pupils "—they're offering more money, Sky. They say you have a real following in these adventure films, and they're willing to pay us bigger money to capitalize on that."

"You have to spend money to make money," Sky mused, idly mixing the cards.

"That's the name of the game, Sky. It'll happen for you. You'll get what you want. We'll be patient, play the game. We're building here, boy, building a career for you brick by brick."

Elaina watched Sky consider the offer. It was almost like watching him fall backward over the edge of the trail.

"I won't be on my feet for several months," he reported absently.

"They know that. They say they can work with that. At this point, the production schedule is flexible."

"Even then, I may limp for a while."

O'Malley's eyes narrowed. "You're not staying here for all this surgery, are you? We'll get you out to L.A., where we've got a little more to choose from in the way of—"

Sky's attention seemed to be on the cards. Whatever hand he was being dealt, he'd play it out. There was a lot to consider now, more than he'd been dealing with just a few short weeks ago. He answered without looking up. "I plan to be back on the coast as soon as Elaina...well, as soon as we make some plans. I want her with me. Maybe a week. Tell them to give me a week to think about it."

Elaina wondered what Sky saw in those cards. What plans? How would she fit in?

"Sky, these people have been waiting—"

Sky looked up now, and his dark eyes offered no alternatives. "One week, O'Malley. Tell them I was heavily sedated when you talked to me."

O'Malley felt he had his answer. "Take care, then, boy. You take care of him, Elaina." He pushed his chair back to the wall. "I can't tell you how much it pleases me to see him with a nice girl for a change."

There was a long silence after O'Malley left. Elaina studied her hands, and Sky lit a cigarette. He watched the gray-white cloud float toward the ceiling.

"You're considering this contract, then?" Elaina asked quietly.

"I can be looking for something else while I do this." He didn't look at her. He didn't believe it, either.

"It isn't what you want," she reminded him.

"No, but it's a damn good living." He turned to her now, and she let him see the disappointment in her eyes. "I can play any part they hand me if you'll go with me, Elaina. Be part of my life."

"Whether I'm with you or not, you can't be someone you don't want to be. Who are you? Sky? Dan? Who am I talking to?"

"What difference does the name make?" he demanded. "You know who I am. You've seen the best and the worst of me."

"Have I?" She moved to the bed and sat on the edge, because she felt she belonged there. He needed to see where she was. She wanted to be with him, and he'd asked her to be part of his life, but she wondered what part. What life. "I haven't seen you playing a part you didn't like. I haven't seen you running around with women who mean nothing to you, or using those 'painkillers' you mentioned to get rid of some pain of your own making."

The fervor drained from his eyes, and they became cold, black hollows. He took a long drag of his cigarette before he stubbed it out, staring through her. "That's all over," he told her, his voice ominously low. "No one will ever see me that way again."

"But if you give in to this, Sky, if you play the same role again . . ." She felt an awful burning rising in her throat.

"I told you those things because I trusted you to know them and not use them against me. That's my baggage, not yours."

"Then set it aside and be the man you want to be. I won't—"

Voices in the hallway interrupted them for a second time. Elaina recognized Joe Two Moon's deep, smooth voice and Jenny's bossy response. A second woman entered the room with them. She was tall and stout, her dark hair coarse and shiny, like Sky's, and her face was identifiably that of his mother.

"You must be the woman who refused to abandon my son," the woman said, offering her hand. "I'm Ramona Sky Hunter."

After a few moments of polite conversation Elaina decided that this was Sky's family's time, not hers. She moved to his bedside and bent for a soft, bittersweet kiss. "I'm going home," she whispered. "If you get a chance, call me." Then she kissed him again as she pressed something into his hand.

"Elaina!" he called, but she was gone before he fully understood that she was leaving. He opened his hand and looked down at the small, gold heart and its chain.

Chapter Twelve

Mid-October had turned cold in Minneapolis, which came as no surprise to the residents. After Labor Day most people had closed their lake cottages and dry-docked their boats for the winter. Summer was always a short season, cherished all the more because it flew by so quickly. By September the vacations were over, the memories filed in photograph albums, and winter was imminent. What autumn there was had come in September and was already slipping away, notch by notch, on the October thermometer. Little was left on the trees, their brown leaves huddling against brick walls in brittle piles like the colorless negatives of those summer photographs.

Elaina had no photographs. Her camera, along with the rest of her personal possessions, had been dumped off the back of a terrified horse somewhere on a mountain in Wyoming. She had memories, though, and they haunted her daily. There had been no phone call. When her pride had drained away weeks earlier, she'd called the hospital in Billings, but of course he'd left. She'd called Silver Moon simply to inquire about how his surgery had gone, but Jenny knew very little. "He never writes, never calls," Jenny complained. "That's the way he is. One day he just shows up for a visit. You'll see him when you see him, so don't be surprised."

She only needed to hear his voice, Elaina told herself. She needed to know that he was all right, that the series of operations had gone well and there would be no permanent damage. Because they'd come through the ordeal together, she had a stake in his recovery. For her part, she was recovering nicely. She only thought of him . . . a few times during the day, just before she fell asleep at night, and every minute that she slept.

Elaina cradled a huge Persian cat while she viewed the lights of the city from her apartment window. She could see the University of Minnesota across the river, and beyond that the lights of St. Paul. Lately she'd been thinking of moving into the suburbs, maybe Eden Prairie or Brooklyn Park. She would like a little less city around her, she thought. She wanted to build a fire, even if it had to be in a fireplace, and she wanted to be able to put a big plastic moose in her front yard. Or at least the back. She was entitled to her eccentricities; she was a writer, after all.

She'd wandered away from her computer with the excuse of making herself a cup of tea. If she didn't get her act together, she wouldn't be able to call herself a writer much longer. Her pack trip story wasn't going well. The guide kept turning into the main character. He was too witty, too sexy, too exciting to be a secondary character, especially a villain. She would write him out of a scene, but he'd sneak right back in. She'd almost decided to give him his own book and see if the catharsis of writing it would cure her wishful thinking.

There was always a strange surge of wishful thinking each time she heard a knock at the door. Elaina checked the clock on the buffet as she set the cat on the floor. Nine-fifteen. Nighttime visitors were a nuisance, and she'd let all her friends know that. This was her best writing time. Used to be her best writing time, she reminded herself, glancing at the computer on her desk. The blinking cursor was laughing at her.

It was Elaina who did the blinking when she peeked through the tiny peephole. There she stood, wearing a robe and slippers, for heaven's sake, no makeup because she'd showered earlier, her hair an absolute disaster. And there *he* stood, beautiful and as bold as you please.

"Sky, what a sur—"

"You're supposed to say, 'Who is it?' before you open the door." He wasn't smiling, but she thought she detected an almost hopeful gleam in his eye, as though he hadn't been quite sure he would be allowed admittance. He looked as though he had rested in the care of some attentive nurse, who'd seen that he ate properly and got plenty of sunshine. His blue-black hair was swept across his forehead and curled over the nape of his neck as though styled by a lucky accident.

Elaina pushed her hair back at the temple, finger-combing it in an unconscious bid for improvement. She just wanted to look at him and listen to the rich, low tone of his voice, but she said, "I have a viewer. I could see..."

"You're supposed to ask anyway, so I can tell you who I am. It's customary."

She just wanted to look at him, because she'd never seen him dressed this way, almost unnaturally handsome in a light blue shirt and tie, and a wheat-colored suit with squarely-tailored shoulders that were the icing on an already sweet cake. To please him, she managed, "Who is it?"

His smile came slowly, brightening his eyes. "It's Dan Sky Hunter."

The look on his face did it more than anything. His face was alive with pure pleasure. Her throat went dry. "Until I get used to the change, do you mind if I call you Sky?"

"You can call me any damn thing you please if you're as glad to see me—" she filled his arms, slipping her hands under his jacket to hug him close

"—as I am to see you. You just stood there, and I wasn't sure."

"I wasn't, either. I'd given up on you." She closed her eyes and breathed the smell of him. There was cologne, which wasn't part of her memory, but underneath there was Sky.

"I find that hard to believe," he murmured into her hair. "You didn't before." Ah, that delicious smell of coconut. He'd looked for it once in a store and hadn't been able to find quite the right formula. He decided what was missing was the cornsilk of Elaina's hair.

"That was different. I couldn't give up. All you had was me up there."

He groaned, remembering. "All you had was me, and what a pair we made. I hate to tell you this, honey, but I still need to sit down and put my foot up."

Elaina drew back to look at the only left ankle in all the world she considered to be worthy of countless hours of mental anguish. It was bound in a walking cast. "Come in, and let me... Did you just get here? Can I get you something to eat? Let me take your jacket."

Recovering the crutch he'd propped against the wall in the hallway, he came inside. She closed the front door and took a hanger from the entryway closet, but he shook his head when he spotted the living room. "No, thanks. I'll wear the jacket. All I need is a sofa and a hassock." He found both and made himself comfortable.

The apartment, from what he saw of it, was efficient as she was, neat but lived-in, and tastefully appointed. The colors were muted—navy, mauve and silver. There was a print of a Plains Indian on one wall, one of a white cat on another. Bookshelves lined a third wall, and they were well-stocked. There was nothing frilly or overtly feminine about the decor, but it felt as though a woman lived there. It felt as though Elaina lived there, and Sky didn't care if he never saw the inside of his own apartment again. He wondered what her bedroom was like.

"How has your surgery gone?" she asked, joining him on the end of her plush navy sofa, which was covered with white cat hair. Why hadn't he given her half an hour's warning?

"I've had three operations, and they think that might be the end of it. I had the third one a week and a half ago. I'm walking on it a couple of days before I was supposed to."

"Oh, Sky..."

He shrugged and gave her a sheepish grin. "I couldn't wait any longer. I wanted to see you."

"Why didn't you call me?" she asked. They sat knee to knee, and she touched his tentatively with just three fingers.

"I wanted to come to you. I didn't want you watching me coming out of surgery, going back into surgery, always being wheeled around from room to room. I wanted to walk through your door." He'd had plenty of time to dream about it, to block out the scene in his mind. He always caught her by surprise, dressed just as she was now, and she always looked natural, just as she had in the mountains. There was no more pink sunburn, but the summer sun highlights still graced her yellow hair, and her face was polished ivory.

"It's all fixed, then?" The question was pitched high with hope.

"I have a pin in my ankle, but they think it'll function normally. They tell me it was like a jigsaw puzzle that had to be pieced back together." He covered her hand with his. "Now tell me how *you* are, Elaina. Any ill effects from our... little adventure?"

"Some effects, perhaps, but nothing ill." She looked down at his hand and saw that he wore a ring on his little finger with a small gold heart at its center. She touched the heart carefully.

"It was all you left me," he said. "I took it as a gift, and I wanted to wear it."

"It was a gift." Her voice wouldn't come out strong and steady, the way she wanted it to.

"What effects, Elaina? Are you... pregnant?"

"No," she said, too quickly.

"I wouldn't mind if you were." She glanced up, her blue eyes wide with surprise, and he smiled. "I know I told you I wouldn't give my wife a baby, but I'll give you as many as you want. Just say the word."

Not my wife, but I'll give you... What would her status be? "Sky, I'm not in the market for..."

"I'm getting ahead of myself." He raised his palm to back himself up a step. "I came as a suitor."

"A suitor?"

"A suitor," he repeated, then ran his lapel between his thumb and forefinger. "See the suit?"

"Yes, I do, and would you just look at me?" She pulled the front of her blue velour robe away from her chest in disgust. "Covered with cat hair and wearing my work clothes." He hiked one eyebrow. She raised two and gave a casual shrug. "No matter what kind of work a lady does in the evening, she likes to be comfortable. You could have called from the airport and given me time to get dressed and clean the place up a little."

"Would you have baked a cake?" The boyish grin said he might have liked that.

She brushed at the hair on the cushion between them. "I would've vacuumed, at least. You'll get cat hair all over your suitor's suit."

"Hey, I wanted to surprise you." His hand closed over hers, putting a stop to her ineffective brushing. "I came to see you, and I like what I see. Can you say the same?"

She eyed him from crest to cast, deliberately taking her time. "Nice suit. I've been wondering how you got those pants on over your cast."

"Easy. I'm sewn into them."

"You're what?" She turned a puzzled expression on the cast that was propped on her hassock.

"I went to the shop to pick up the suit before I caught my plane. I had the tailor cut open the seam and sew me into my pants."

"Why?"

He gave her a look of mock exasperation. "Because a suitor has to wear a suit. I've been reading up on this." Reaching inside his breast pocket, he drew out a copy of one of her romances. "I know just how it works now that I've done my research."

This wasn't what she'd imagined whenever she'd dreamed of his coming back to her. In her dreams he was dramatic, not teasing. In her dreams he'd missed her terribly, torn up a hundred letters because none of them said what he felt, had nearly wasted away in agony because each time he'd called there had been no answer. "I have a feeling I'm about to be satirized."

"The highest form of flattery," he assured her as he paged through the book.

"That's imitation."

"Nothing about this scene is imitation, honey. Wait'll you see the…ah, here it is." He pointed to the middle of the page. "You read Tanya, and I'll be Dirk. I've got it memorized."

"You would," she said, submitting reluctantly.

He pointed again. "Go ahead. Start right there."

Elaina sighed and found the spot. "'I won't let you dictate terms, Dirk—'"

"Sky," he corrected. "Dirk is a terrible name."

She tried not to smile. "'I won't let you dictate terms, Sky. You keep telling me what you want, but you never hear what I want.'"

"'What do you want?'"

"'I want a man who isn't afraid to tell me what he feels. I want a man who's willing to *show* some feeling. Maybe even shed an honest tear once in a while.'"

"I can cry on cue," Sky confided in a whisper. "We could add that in."

Elaina laughed and rolled her eyes. "Just read it the way it's written, Mr. Hunter."

"Okay, okay." He drew a small box from his pocket and opened it. Elaina's eyes widened, and Sky laughed. "Very good, honey, that's just what it says, see—" he pointed to the text and read "—'He drew a small box from his pocket and opened it.' Great expression, Elaina. Now my line is, 'Does this show you anything about my feelings?'"

"Sky, you can't just . . ."

"No, she doesn't say that. She says . . ."

"Sky—" Elaina closed the book. "You've never said anything about marriage. If that's what the ring is for . . ."

"Of course it's what the ring is for." His voice became tentative as he held his proposal out to her. "Don't you like it?"

Taking the box from his hand, she brought the teardrop diamond close to her breast.

"They didn't have a heart-shaped one," he told her shyly. "I looked."

"It's beautiful, Sky," she whispered.

"Do you need some time to think about it? I'll wait." He couldn't see her eyes, and that bothered him. He always took so much pleasure in her eyes. "How many minutes do you need?"

"What did you decide . . . about your career?"

The question came as a series of rasps, and he ached to hold her. "I turned the offer down." The announcement was made with the same deliberateness he'd used in accomplishing the deed. He'd considered the contract, reread the script, and finally flatly refused. "I got a new agent."

She snapped the box closed and looked up quickly. Her eyes had become azure with unshed tears and wide with some unnamed fear. "Because of what I said?"

"Because you reminded me of what I've been saying for a long time. I can do better."

"I had no right to make those comments, Sky. What do I know about the movie business?" The small velvet box reminded her of a little flocked toy, the kind she'd collected as a child. She rubbed it with her thumb the same way she had the bear whose face had finally worn no features at all.

"You told me your name, and I didn't tell you mine," she continued softly. "It's not Delacourte; it's Delaney. Elaina Delaney." Emboldened by her burst of honesty, she sniffed, swiped at her tears and made a feeble joke. "It sounds like a limerick, doesn't it? I changed it because I didn't like the sound of it." Casting a sigh to the ceiling, she shook her head and tried again. "And because I didn't want to be the girl whose husband walked out on her before the marriage even got started."

"You took your maiden name back right away didn't you?" he asked, telling himself that that boy had had no claim on her. He'd never had the backbone she deserved in a man. Sky hoped he had it.

"The marriage was annulled," she reminded him. "It never happened. He took my maidenhood and left me my maiden name." After all this time it sounded foolish when she said it aloud, and she laughed. "Sounds like something out of a medieval romance, doesn't it? I've actually let that rejection dig at me for a long, long time."

"Too long." She nodded, and he put his hand over both of hers. "And you were too young," he pointed out. "Neither one of you was ready for marriage. You probably fell into it like I did—at a time when my hormones were driving me crazy and the girl I figured I belonged with was looking for a way to get out from under her mother's roof."

"In my case, there was another complication."

"You got pregnant when you were still a child. It happens." She glanced up, surprised by the way he summed it up so simply, so well. "And you got married too soon. *That* happens. I did it, too. I wasn't any more ready for marriage than I was for liver paté back then."

Her smile came slowly, her eyes full of sparkling tears. "Liver paté?"

"Sure. Just because it leaves a bitter taste in your mouth the first time you try it doesn't mean it won't become a delicacy somewhere down the road."

"So what am I?" she asked, laughing through sweet tears. "Chopped liver?"

"You're gourmet fare, honey, and it's taken me a while, but I've acquired a gourmet palate. We're ready for this now—both of us. Elaina Sky Hunter doesn't sound like a limerick, does it?"

"No," she said softly. "It sounds lovely."

"You love me, Elaina. I know that as surely as I know I love you."

"Yes, Sky," she said, her voice taking on new strength. She wanted to share in the conviction in his eyes. "I do love you. But you're trying to get away from stereotypes, and I create them...because they're safe. Because they're predictable. Because they can't go off and leave me with a hand full of annulment papers."

"My God, Elaina, that all happened a long time ago. A lifetime ago. You told me to put my baggage aside. Now take your own advice. You've become a good writer, and people enjoy your books." He lifted her chin in his hands and drew his thumbs across her cheeks to dry her tears. "If you want to write better Indian characters, I suggest you get to know one very, very well."

"Is one enough?" she asked, taking a quick swipe at another tear. "I probably should get to know a cross section, you know, for the sake of good resear—"

He held her face still in his hands and dropped a hard kiss over her suggestion. He'd waited a long time for this kiss, and it couldn't be soft, wouldn't be gentle. The tip of his tongue found hers to tell her just how hard the waiting had been. He left her breathless when he drew back and quietly assured her, "One is enough."

"It may take some time."

"Time for what?"

"I want to know Dan Sky Hunter," she whispered.

His dark eyes bored into hers with a promise that was more intense than the one he spoke aloud to her. "I can't promise you'll like everything you get to know about him, but I promise you one thing. If I can get your name on that marriage license, you won't be left with any annulment papers."

They shared a kiss that burned Elaina from her lips to her chest. Part of the sensation came from the tears she'd swallowed and part from the way everything inside her strained to reach out to him. When he kissed her, all things seemed possible, and when he drew back again, the look on his face said that all things were.

"What about your career?" she asked in a tentative whisper. "O'Malley said you might not find—"

"Marcus and Leed isn't the only agency in town. I thought about taking the offer because it was good money. I wanted to offer you all the things money could buy, but you made me see things a little differently when you told me to be the man I wanted to be. I found a risk worth taking."

"You got another offer?"

He nodded, sliding his hands over her shoulders. "It's a new production company owned by a prominent Indian businessman. He thinks there's room on the market for Indian actors in quality films. And we agree with him, don't we?"

"Yes, we do," she ventured, hooking her hands over his forearms.

"He gave me a script, and I read it when I was in the hospital. It's a story about people, Elaina." His eyes burned with excitement, and Elaina's enthusiasm was ignited by his. "I play a man whose daughter is a runaway. A real *man*, Elaina, not a caricature."

"It's what you really wanted, then."

"It's not as much money, but, yeah, it's what I really wanted. So if you'd consider marrying a struggling actor rather than a stereotypical hero, I think you'll get a man somewhere in the bargain."

She smiled. "You'll still end up with a romantic woman."

"Some of those romantic notions aren't really half bad. I'm not sure how you combine the guy with the feelings with the hard man of few words, but I like the way he gets her into the bedroom before the book ends." He put his arms around her. "I didn't take the time to get a room at a hotel."

"Hmm." With deft fingers she loosened the knot of his tie. "You mean I get this bargain of a man tonight?"

"If you agree to wear my ring." She smiled her agreement, and he took the box from her lap and slipped the ring onto her finger.

"It fits," she marveled, sliding her hand up his lapel as she slanted it toward the light to admire the ring.

"I should be a director. The whole scene went perfectly, right down to the size of the ring."

"We just have one more problem."

He was nuzzling her ear, which made her wonder whether there could be any problem at hand actually worth mentioning.

"What's that, honey?"

"Your pants are sewn on."

He leaned back and reached into his pocket, drawing out the pocket knife he'd always found a thousand uses for. He handed it to her with a look that challenged her imagination. "I leave that problem in your inventive hands."

She reached for his belt buckle, and he heard music in his head when she smiled her unmistakable promise.

*   *   *   *   *

NOVEMBER TITLES

SOME WARM HUNGER
Bay Matthews

ALL THINGS CONSIDERED
Debbie Macomber

CHASE THE WIND
Rebecca Swan

SNOWBOUND
Lisa Jackson

TREASURES OF THE HEART
Anne Lacey

CARVED IN STONE
Kathleen Eagle

Silhouette Special Edition

COMING NEXT MONTH

BREAKING EVERY RULE
Victoria Pade

Of all the scary things in the world, novelist Kelsey
McKenna feared publicity most. A woman who'd
broken every rule, she now had to confront her past.
TV star Thomas Quinn-Patrick Sullivan was
pursuing not only the screen rights to her book, but
also Kelsey herself. Could she keep him at a
distance?

SUMMERTIME BLUES
Natalie Bishop

After fourteen years Tanner Baines was back in
Portland, and the sultry Oregon summer reminded
Maggie of the passion they had briefly shared... and
a love she could not forget. Would things be
different this time?

THE MAN BEHIND THE BADGE
Paula Hamilton

Courtney's interviews with police negotiator Mike
Harris were interesting, but privately she admitted
this was more than just a story. Off duty Mike kept
his feelings well hidden; could Courtney ever
uncover the man behind the badge?

Silhouette Special Edition

COMING NEXT MONTH

SOLITAIRE
Lindsay McKenna

Another super book featuring the Kincaid family!
Cat Kincaid is deeply indebted and attracted to
Slade Donovan, but would risking her life earn
merely his gratitude?

LOVE CAN MAKE IT BETTER
Allyson Ryan

Jennifer Hamilton, child psychologist
extraordinaire, found counseling teenagers on the
birds and bees a picnic compared to tangling with Dr
Trevor Hawke. Their passion was mutual, but their
aims were not... surely two adults could work out a
solution?

A VISION TO SHARE
Jillian Blake

Kate was dazzled by Nick's energy and charm. He
was equally impressed by her tranquility. But Nick
had a few skeletons in his closet... were they going to
upset the applecart?

MJ0865

Silhouette
Special Edition Romances

YOU'RE INVITED TO ACCEPT
4 SPECIAL
EDITION ROMANCES
AND A TOTE BAG
FREE!

Acceptance card

| NO STAMP NEEDED | Post to: **Silhouette Reader Service, FREEPOST, P.O. Box 236, Croydon, Surrey. CR9 9EL** |

Please note readers in Southern Africa write to:
Independent Book Services P.T.Y., Postbag X3010, Randburg 2125, S. Africa

YES! Please send me 4 free Silhouette Special Edition Romances and my free tote bag – and reserve a Reader Service Subscription for me. If I decide to subscribe I shall receive 6 new Special Edition Romances each month as soon as they come off the presses for £7.50 together with a FREE monthly newsletter including information on top authors and special offers, exclusively for Reader Service subscribers. There are no postage and packing charges, and I understand I may cancel or suspend my subscription at any time. Even if I decide not to subscribe the 4 free novels and the tote bag are mine to keep forever.
I am over 18 years of age.

mps EP28SE

NAME _____

(CAPITALS PLEASE)

ADDRESS _____

_____

_____ POSTCODE _____

The right is reserved to refuse an application and change the terms of this offer. You may be mailed with other offers as a result of this application. Offer expires March 31st 1988 and is limited to one per household.
Offer applies in UK and Eire only. Overseas send for details.